The Transparent Pearl

Alison Lewis

© 2002**Alison Lewis**

## Preface

The play starts at a future welfare office in America. Due to economic hardship in America, the welfare office is not just for the poor but visited by the working middle class, and the college educated. The office processes intakes for welfare housing and services, and also houses the only medical clinic in the area. The former welfare services: Medicaid, food stamps, cash assistance, rent assistance, daycare, and Medicaid transportation no longer exist. The SSI system has also crashed, the government is no longer able to pay SSI checks, so services for the "mentally disabled" are administered through the new welfare system.

  *The characters in this play are fictional, and this play is not based on any real-life events or real people

## Act 1: Fall
Scene 1: October: Welfare Intake Office Q, a day of introductions
Scene 2: October: Welfare Intake Office Q, a few days later
Scene 3: November: Macy's Department Store Welfare Housing site, a few days later

## Act 2: Winter
Scene 1: January: Documentary prescreening dinner
Scene 2: February: Welfare Intake Office  Q, a dreary Friday

## Act 3: Spring
Scene 1: March: Welfare Intake Office Q, a Friday, a day of awakening
Scene 2: April: A Saturday morning, a coffee shop and museum
Scene 3: May: Welfare Intake Office Q, a Monday morning, a day of encounters

## Act 4: Summer
Scene 1: June: A Saturday, the importance of the moment
Scene 2: July: Welfare Intake Office Q, a hot and humid Wednesday
Scene 3: Late August: Ryan and Marie's wedding
### Epilogue: Fall, October 2002

# Characters

Casting note: People of any cultural background can be cast in all main or minor roles, except the narrator should be cast as an Afro-American young male, age twenty-two to thirty.

Narrator—This individual is invisible to the main characters. Some minor characters in the story recognize the narrator as a person but do not converse with him or realize he is talking about them. The children interact with the narrator in the welfare intake waiting room.

## Staff at Welfare Intake Office Q
Roy Blunt—Director
Pearl Wood—Welfare Intake counselor
James Markus—Medical Director (called "Dr. Mark" and "James" throughout the play)
Jane Bidding—Referral Specialist Supervisor
Claire Smith—Placement Supervisor
Ryan Little—State accountant
Mike Scott--Medical assistant to Dr. James Markus
Mary Jones—The intern
Other welfare staff: Rosy, Stella

## Clients and Visitors at Welfare Intake Office Q
Bob Parker—Client
Joan Baxter—Client
Ronald P. Johnson—Client
Margaret Brown—Client
John Roberts —Client
Rita Ballington—Wealthy female visitor
Luke Matthews—*Times Today* news reporter

**Others**

Beatrice—Pearl's friend at the coffee shop/museum

Ms. Anne—Pearl's elderly neighbor

Marie—Ryan's fiancé

Nurse practitioner at Macy's Department Store Welfare Housing site

Anthony—Elementary-school-age boy at Macy's Department Store Welfare Housing site

Lauren—Luke's date

Young James—Age six to eight

Young Luke—Age eight

Young Pearl—Ages four and five

Pearl's father/mother

James's mother

James's nanny

Young boys with Young Luke

Homeless drunk man in Kansas City, Missouri

Film director, sponsors and speaker at the prescreening documentary dinner

Extra children and adults for the welfare intake waiting area and department store welfare placement site

Extra people and wait staff at museums/restaurants/art shows

**Act 1, scene 1: October: Welfare Intake Office Q, a day of introductions**

*Black stage, song softly playing in the background Solomon, Hans Zimmer.*
*A spotlight appears on Bob Parker, who is standing in the middle of the empty stage; his hat is in front of him on the ground to collect tips. He's talking to himself and scribbling notes on torn pieces of dirty paper. He's a man in his fifties, his appearance seems neat looking but he's not consistently groomed. He's wearing a worn, dark suit blazer with dress pants and dress shoes.*

Bob Parker: *(head is down, shaking no)* No, no, that's not right. *(mumbles to himself and then peers out with his hand at his forehead toward the audience and yells out)* America? *(pauses and yells with desperation)* Are you listening to me? *(scribbles on paper and looks up with seriousness)*

*Stage lights down.*
*Stage lights up.*
*Set of Welfare Intake Office Q, music fades away after set appears and when narrator begins to speak.*

*The waiting room of Welfare Intake Office Q. On stage are gray chairs that curve around in uneven and unorganized rows. A faded, worn square carpet serves as a children's area. There are a few scattered toys around on the carpet. There are some freestanding whiteboards that are blank and randomly placed on stage/used as screens to project information on during the play. There are framed free standing clear front doors towards the back of the stage. Towards the front center of the stage, there is a staff counter, and behind the counter are framed large freestanding green glass double doors. On the other side of the double green glass doors are* scattered small desks and chairs to create an office look, and some desks placed by themselves to be imagined as offices.

Narrator: *(looking at a ten-year-old child slowly rolling a yellow plastic school bus back and forth, in rhythmic way)* I've seen her here before. Doesn't she seem rather old to be entertained by this toy? *(pauses)* Is she soothed by the back and forth motion? *(pauses)* She seems comfortable. Well, we all need something to soothe us.

Narrator: (*gestures at a few clients sitting in the chairs*) It's not usually this quiet. *(fluorescent light flickering out)* This lighting is annoying. (*breathes in and makes a distasteful face*) The air is stagnant in here. I feel suffocated.

*The narrator walks towards the staff counter area where Pearl is standing and reading a laptop.*

Narrator: (*reads a sign*) Welfare Counselor. *(stands in front of the staff counter area and gestures at the counter)* Well, I feel intimidated now. *(points at double green glass doors).* Oh, look at those doors. *He approaches the doors, gesturing at the doors as if they are enormous.* Look at these *large* double-glass, green-tinted doors. These are powerful doors. They lock this world *(gestures to the clients in waiting area)* away from the world behind those doors.

*Narrator walks over and peers through the green glass doors. A spotlight appears on welfare workers sitting at small desks. The sound of voices begins. The staff speak into little microphones, all talking over each other but in a rhythmic way, saying financial information, education, and work histories.*

Narrator: The welfare staff. Hear'em loading people's lives into audio files? Like they're just telling stories. Like they aren't real people. (*pause*) And, yeah, no paper files anymore. Can you imagine no paper files in a welfare office?

*The narrator steps back from the green glass doors as Claire approaches from the other side. Claire leans out of one of the green glass doors.*

Claire Smith: Pearl?

*Claire's character freezes in the scene.*
*The main characters also freeze in the scene. A keyboard is rolled out onstage.*

Narrator: Pearl Wood, age twenty-six. *(approaches Pearl and gestures at her)* She looks naïve and unworldly. (*makes a negative face*) Oh, (*whispers loudly*) and she's shy. (*pause*) But, wait, I missed something. She has a hidden quality. (*gestures as if something is radiating from her*) A quality that defines her—actually a quite desirable quality. (*pauses, makes a dismissive face*) It's really hard to see though.

*Narrator at the keyboard and starts playing the keyboard while he talks.*

Narrator: We all have a hidden quality. It's inside us, pushed forward by an invisible force. Yes, an *invisible* force. No, this is not a science-fiction story. Invisible force, get it?
*Narrator laughs and plays a well-known science-fiction music theme [Star Wars] on the keyboard. (serious tone*) Wait, where was I?

*Narrator leaves the keyboard and walks around the people in the waiting-room chairs. The people look at him and smile, but they don't respond to his talking.*

Narrator: Invisible force. An invisible force that silently screams out *(with emphasis on each word)* who we really are. *(Narrator points at a man sitting quietly by himself.)* Here's a man who was in prison for five years for selling drugs. Do you see his hidden quality? *(studies him)* I see it!

*Narrator walks over to another person in the waiting room. The person is nodding out on drugs.*

What about this man?! Yeah, he's high on heroin. But what else do you see? Well, don't bother if you can't see it. *(Sigh)* Some are just better at seeing it. *(Narrator smiles and nods at Pearl).*

*Narrator returns to the keyboard and begins playing dramatic notes, pounding on the keyboard.*

Narrator: Conquer! Conquer! Conquer! *(laughs)* Well, not in the barbaric sense.

*Narrator gets up and writes big and expressively the word "Conquer" on a free standing whiteboard.* These old whiteboards haven't been touched in years. Who the hell needs a whiteboard anymore? *(pauses and then paces back and forth and points to the word "Conquer")*

Now, if you can conquer in America, you get lots of attention. Tons of attention. And, it doesn't matter what your hidden quality is. Nope, not if you can conquer. What's conquering in America? Its status. Its power. Its money. *(pauses and writes status, power, money)* The American dream! Yes, the American Dream! *(writes American Dream)*

*(Nods his head and points at Pearl)* Pearl has no idea how to conquer.

*Narrator puts down the marker as the front doors open. Luke Matthews walks in. Narrator returns to the keyboard and starts playing it again.*

Narrator: Conquer! (*directed at Luke as he walks across the stage towards the staff counter*) Luke Matthews, age twenty-eight. He knows how to conquer. See it? Look at that confident walk and commanding personality. No shyness there. He's headed for the American Dream alright. (*pause*) Wait, I think there's something missing in him. (*pause*) Well, who cares if he's missing something? He has what it takes to succeed, to reach the American dream! That's all that matters.

*Narrator leaves the keyboard and plops into a waiting-room chair as if tired; the chair is facing the staff area.*

Narrator: (*cradles his face in his hands*) OK, enough existential philosophy. I feel a headache coming on. (*points at Claire and rolls his eyes*) Back to the story.

*The characters unfreeze, and the scene continues.*

Claire: (*more demanding*) Pearl!

*Pearl's head is down as she is reading on a laptop.*

Pearl: (*timidly*) Yes?

Claire: (*abruptly*) Here (*drops a computer tablet by Pearl*). They're all going to the Macy's housing site. Check their medical clearance.

*Before Pearl responds to Claire, Luke Matthews approaches and interrupts.*

Luke: (*very commanding approach and serious in his expressions, very emotionless tone*) Hi. Luke Matthews with the *Times Today*. I'm here to take notes for the documentary. Where can I start?

Claire: (*speaks rudely*) Documentary? I have no idea what you're talking about. *Claire begins to reopen the green glass doors.* Wait here.

Luke: OK, it's set. But if you must check, speed it up, I have a deadline. (*smiles but in a commanding, expressionless way*) *Claire becomes more attentive to Luke before letting the doors shut.*

Narrator: (*raises his arm*) Conquer!

*Luke takes a seat in the waiting area and begins working on a small computer tablet. As Pearl glances up from her work she notices Luke sitting in the chair.*

Narrator: (*gestures and points to Luke sitting among the clients*) Noticeable difference.

*Pearl turns around when she hears loud talking from behind the green glass doors. Narrator approaches the green glass doors and peers in.*

Narrator: Oh, coffee break time.

*Scene moves to behind the green glass doors; a stage light focuses on the welfare workers standing around each other, drinking coffee.*

Rosey: Complaints, complaints, complaints. (*sips her coffee*) I'm tired of it. It's not our fault there are no good housing placements. And, I can't listen to one more complaint about the Macy's housing site. (*rolls her eyes*) Ugh.

Stella: (*holds her coffee mug up in the air as she talks*) If they don't like the placements, they need to get off their asses and make some money. Take care of their children. What's wrong with these people? They just don't get it.

Rosey: They need to stop the drugs and booze. Just say no, people. That slogan's been around for decades. Don't they get it? Guess not, since the same damn ones keep coming back.

*Stage lights fade on the scene and return to the waiting room.*

*Narrator walks away from the green glass doors and pulls out a guitar from a nearby corner and starts strumming it. As the scene continues, we see children slowly gather around the narrator while he plays, and clients are entering through the front doors and sitting in waiting area.*
*Luke approaches Pearl. Luke speaks in a very commanding and emotionally disconnected tone.*

Luke: *(reads sign)* Welfare counselor? What's your name?

Pearl: *(hesitant by Luke's forward nature, she quickly becomes noticeably timid and avoids some eye contact.)* Pearl.

Luke: (*says very directly, dry and not with much emotion*) What do you do?
*Luke turns on his phone to record.*

Pearl: Well, Claire didn't come back yet.

Luke: *(firmly)* Really? Why would I waste my time?

Pearl: *(hesitates. Holds up a computer tablet.)* I'll show you the general stuff. I give out the welfare intake forms. People come here for two reasons. Either to see Dr. Mark or for welfare housing placement services.

Luke: So what are some of the forms like?
*She points her tablet to a white board, and the forms appear. She speaks quickly at first.*

Pearl:  These are required for everyone; permission to search bank accounts, work history, assets, properties, even pre-purchased burial plots. Here's the one for the social and family history.

Luke: That's five pages?

Pearl: Yeah, it's long. *(new form appears)* But this one, the wage agreement form, is only required for a welfare housing placement. You have to sign over your wages to pay for your welfare housing services. Well, except for your wage stipend.

Luke: What's a wage stipend?

Pearl: It's the weekly wages that you get to keep. About one percent of your wages. Basically nothing. Oh, but, if you have a lot of work history and education you can get a higher wage stipend. Maybe three or four percent of your weekly earnings.

*Slowly Pearl becomes less timid. Luke continues with questions in a robotic and focused manner.*

Luke: Ok, so the forms get completed, then what?

Pearl: Well, if they want medical services they wait to see Dr. Mark, or get an appointment to come back.  If they want a welfare housing placement, they're sent to a site at the end of the day. Most get sent to the Macy's Department Store communal housing site, but some go to the JC Penny site. The vans come at the end of the day and bring them.

Luke: Didn't I read there are other housing sites? Besides the department store sites?

Pearl: Yeah, boarding houses, and apartments. But they're hard to get.

*The green glass doors open and interrupt them.*

Claire: Mr. Matthews, you can proceed. *Claire glances with frustration at Pearl.* I guess you already started with Pearl. *(gives list to Luke)* Here's a list of other staff members. Mr. Blunt might be available later. He's the director of this office.

Luke: *(curtly)* Thank you. *Claire disappears behind the closing green glass door.* OK. *(glances at his notes, unemotional and disconnected from the information he is collecting)* So does this new welfare system work?

Pearl: *(stammers a bit)* I don't know. The government says it works. But it isn't a fair system.

Luke: *(speaks quickly)* Why?

Pearl: *(stammers a bit)* People can't manage their own wages, sound fair? They have to depend on a residence to provide all their basic needs, clothing, medical care. That's fair?

Luke: *(not looking up, recording on his phone)* Ok, what else?

*A banging noise is heard by the front doors. Luke turns around to see what Pearl is looking at. A woman struggles past the front doors with a small child wrapped in blankets in her arms. Pearl quickly approaches the woman.*

Woman: Please, por favor, sir, ma'am, need help. Baby sick, valor. Hablo español?

Pearl: Un momento. *(picks up phone as the woman spoke)*

*Pearl directs the woman to a chair. The child is softly crying. Pearl walks to get a pillow for the child.*

Narrator: *(looks up from the guitar and stops strumming while he talks)* Ah, the world of the media. There's pressure to get the story no matter how uncomfortable the circumstances. Time is money in the media world.
*Narrator starts strumming again on guitar.*

Luke: (*approaches Pearl, determined to get another question answered*) Why not send her to the hospital? The child might need a hospital.

Pearl: (*polite but seems frustrated with Luke in a passive-aggressive way*) These people can't go to the hospital without approval from Dr. Mark. Another loss of freedom with the new welfare system. *Pearl returns to attend to the woman and hands her the small pillow.* Here's a pillow for your daughter.

*Dr. James Markus comes through the green glass doors. James engages the woman in a brief conversation in spanish. James takes the child in his arms and heads towards the green glass doors.*

James*: (to Pearl but Luke can hear)* The mom said they're at the JC Penny site. She doesn't want to go back; there was a fight last night. She's afraid for herself and her daughter. Oh, and yesterday, the housing daycare staff ignored her daughter's fever, and didn't tell the mom till she got home from work.

*James goes through the glass doors with mother and child.*
*Luke sits in a chair and reviews his notes; he seems disconnected*
*from the events going on around him. Many clients have entered the*
*scene. Some clients' and their children have used clothing but are*
*neat and tidy in appearance; other clients' and kids appear in worn*
*clothing and not groomed. There are children of all ages running*
*around. There are a few single adults sitting by themselves. A few of*
*the adults look like they are sleepy and nodding off as if on drugs.*

Narrator: (*stops playing the guitar, stands up, and places the guitar*
*against a wall*) Look at the children running around. (*smiles and*
*gestures at children, jumping off chairs and running around*)
They've just come from school.

*Luke approaches Pearl again.*

Luke: (*flatly*) It's getting crowded.

Pearl: (*nods yes*)

*Pearl is distracted from her conversation with Luke; there is a line*
*of families at the staff counter trying to ask questions.*

Pearl: (*passively annoyed, she doesn't make eye contact*) You'll have
to wait over there. Or, go find Jane Bidding; she might be able to
speak with you.

Luke: Who's Jane Bidding?

Pearl: She's the referral specialist. (*points to green glass doors*) Go
through these doors and you'll see her.

*Pearl turns away from Luke. Luke gathers his belongings. The narrator follows him. After he passes through the green glass doors, Luke looks over his shoulder at Pearl as if frustrated with getting interrupted.*

*Behind the green glass doors, there is a section of small school sized desks for the welfare staff, and then there are some small scattered office desks on stage, one for Jane, one for Ryan's with a couple free standing file cabinets nearby, and other scattered desks for Mr. Blunt, Claire and Dr. Mark. The freestanding white boards are used as standing screens to project information on.*

*Stage light appears on Jane sitting at a desk by itself to represent an office. Luke knocks on an imaginary door, and leans towards Jane's desk.*

Luke: *(direct and forceful)* Hello. Luke Matthews, *Times Today.* You're the referral specialist?

*Jane is sitting at her desk, and she looks up from her computer. Jane and Luke freeze in the scene while the narrator talks.*

Narrator: Jane Bidding, late fifties. Ready to retire after thirty-plus years as one of the *many* supervisors in state welfare. *Narrator writes on a freestanding whiteboard behind her head: "Accountability."*
*Narrator peeks over Jane's shoulder.* Looks like she's buying a man's shirt. I heard her mention that her husband's birthday was approaching.

*Jane and Luke unfreeze in the scene.*

Jane: Hello! Yes, yes, please come in! *(presents as bubbly, very enthusiastic, appears to be compassionate)* Sit down. *(gestures to the open chair)* I heard all about you *(excitedly talks over Luke and doesn't let him respond)* I'm Jane Bidding. It's about time someone gave a voice to our homeless families. The American people need to understand how we've abandoned our own people. Yes, we are finally moving toward a stable economy, but there's a big part of our population that's not a part of this growth. And why do you think this happened? (*Luke turns on his recording tablet.*) Education. Education has become for the elite. There's a growing population of people who don't have the skills to get the new jobs out there. Where will these people go? We can no longer contain them in boxes and stack them away in a department store.

*Jane glances down at her computer and seems to appear distracted suddenly.*

Luke: (*frustrated and very frank*) What's your role in this welfare housing system?

Jane: I assign the clients to their housing placement. (*Jane speaks fast.*) Level one, Boarding houses. Level two, maybe a boarding house placement but probably a department store placement. Level three, department store placements only.

*Jane appears to be trying to end the conversation. She stands up and is gathering her belongings.*

Luke: (*appears annoyed and confused*) Wait, what did you say? There are levels for assigning welfare housing?

Jane: Yes. Levels. It's called Welfare Economics. All comes down to numbers. The less history you have with welfare services the better your housing placement. Level one—no application history. Level two—at least two years since last application. Level three, or "cycler"—under two years since last application.

Luke: So, level one gets a better housing placement?

Jane: (*ignores Luke*) Well, there really are no guarantees. Anyway, it was great meeting with you. (*very friendly and welcoming* ) I'm always here if you have any questions.

Luke: (*a little frustrated that Jane is leaving so soon*) OK, I'll keep that in mind. (*looks at the staff list*). Can you direct me to Ryan Little?

Jane: (*very bubbly*) Sure, (*points to the right*) (*grabs Luke's hand and shakes it overly excited*) Have a great day! (*smiles and overly exaggerated happy expressions*) And thanks for visiting our office!

*Jane waves bye and rushes off stage.*
*Stage light down on Jane's desk.*
*A stage light appears on Ryan's desk, a screen and a couple free standing file cabinets. Narrator follows Luke to Ryan's desk.*
*Luke pauses to jot down some notes. Both characters freeze as the narrator speaks.*
*Narrator walks towards the file cabinets. He reads the desk name plate.*

Narrator: Ryan Little. (*points to file cabinets.*) Hey, file cabinets! They're never used anymore. (*opens several drawers.*) Oh, look: tons of old paper housing applications. Ha, look at this one! And this one. Is it really that different from this one? (*laughing and aggressively throwing forms on the floor*) This is liberating. I hate these goddamn forms. (*throwing forms on the floor*) OK, yes. (*looking down at the mess of forms*) I should calm down. Back to Ryan. (*closes the file cabinet drawers and straightens his clothes.*) Ryan is a state accountant, age twenty-eight. He has one of the rare state jobs left in social services that offer a decent salary. He wanted to pursue a career as a social worker, but he was afraid to take a risk. Accounting was in his family.
*Narrator moves behind Ryan, folds his arms and becomes quiet.*

Luke: (*approaches Ryan*) Hi.

Ryan: (*looks up from computer*) Hi, (*puts out a hand*) Ryan Little.

Luke: (*shakes hand with his hand*) Luke Matthews from *Times Today*. Did someone mention I was coming to ask you some questions?

Ryan: Ah, yes. Claire told me. Come on in. Sit down.

Luke: So you're an accountant?

Ryan: Yup.

Luke: *(turns on recording computer tablet)* So what do you do?

Ryan: *Ryan laughs. He shows documents, appear on whiteboard.* Too much. I track all the finances of this welfare office and the Macy's site. I monitor client's wages and stipends. Oh, and I can't forget the state statistics database. That's a beast.

Luke: So you manage the client stipends?

Ryan: Well, the computer does most of it. It calculates the client stipend based on the number of months worked, and their education. They don't get much money for themselves.

Luke: Yeah, that's what I heard. What are the financial advantages with this new welfare system?

Ryan: More people work, which means more taxes to pay for the welfare services. American citizens like the new system. They think it cares for the poor and needy without being a burden on their pockets.

*Mrs. Baxter approaches Ryan and does an imaginary knock.*

Ryan:  Hi, Mrs. Baxter, come in. This is Mr. Matthews.

Luke: (*Luke gives a polite but stiff smile*).

Mrs. Baxter: Hello.

Ryan:  He's doing documentary research on the welfare system. Is it ok if he sits in?

Mrs. Baxter:  I don't mind. *(distressed but trying to remain calm)* I'll never get better housing if I can't work. No one wants to hire an elderly woman.

Narrator: Many of the elderly were unable to pay high rents for apartments, and elderly homeowners lost their homes due to rising taxes.

Ryan:  Mrs. Baxter you've been here a few times, but did anyone consider your education level? I see you have an education.

Mrs. Baxter:  No one asked. I have a bachelor's degree. But I don't have much of a work history.  I was a mother most of my life. Why?

Ryan:  The designers of this new welfare system thought that the *un*educated homeless should be separated from the educated homeless. An educated person is entitled to welfare housing advantages. Let me check with Mr. Blunt and see what I can do for you.

Mrs. Baxter: Oh. OK. But this is all so confusing. The forms are so overwhelming. *(distraught)* And what are those levels on that screen? *(points to standing whiteboard screen)*

Ryan: Oh, housing levels. *Ryan turns to standing screen.* Level one—no application history. Level two—at least two years since last application. Level three, or "cycler"—under two years since last application.

Mrs. Baxter: *(worried and fearful)* Does that apply to me? *(points to screen)* Am I assigned a level?

Ryan: Yes, level three. But don't worry Mrs. Baxter; let me look into things.

Mrs. Baxter: OK. *(pauses)* I was living with friends but I had to leave. The house was overcrowded. And I can't stay in those abandoned buildings that people hide out in. Not at my age.

Ryan: *(smiles warmly)* Go stay at the Macy's housing site for now. We'll try to find a different placement real soon.

Mrs. Baxter: Well those sites aren't easy to live at you know? I've tried them before. There are too many people. There are fights. And you always have to wait in line for something. Whether it's to see the nurse, get food, deodorant, even to go to the bathroom. And can't they rename the place? Why do they keep the original store name Macy's? *(pause)* Can't they put some effort into making it more like a home? I use to shop at the Macy's store, you know? I bought my dress for my daughter's wedding there. I never could have imagined I'd be living in an former Macy's department store. *(starts to get tearful)*

Ryan: *(soft smile)* I know. But just for a short time, ok?

*Mrs. Baxter nods and holds back her tears and looks out in the distance.*

Luke: (*very emotionless and is looking at the level system*) Can I ask what does that word "cycler" mean? I keep hearing it.

*Mrs. Baxter continues to gaze as if lost in her thoughts.*

Ryan: Well, you know how people are. *(pauses and lowers his voice)* They like to label the people who never get better and never learn to help themselves. The cyclers are the *frequent flyers*. You know?

Luke: (*without emotion but looks curiously at Mrs. Baxter*) Oh. *(pause)*
*Mrs. Baxter smiles meekly when she notices Luke studying her then Luke looks down at his notes.*
So, if a person doesn't have an education, is there any funding to get one?

Ryan: No. Not anymore. Lawmakers used some statistics to justify cutting the funds. *Ryan's phone rings. Ryan speaks briefly and puts on hold.* Sorry, I have to take this. Mrs. Baxter go see Pearl; she'll help you. Luke, go see if Mr. Blunt is available. *Points to a desk to the right.* Nice to meet you.

*Mrs. Baxter nods a thank you at Ryan and exits stage.*

Luke: Thanks for your time. (*shakes Ryan's hand and leaves*)

*Luke moves towards Mr. Blunt's desk. He's reviewing his notes. The stage lights dim except for a spotlight on Luke and the narrator.*

Narrator: Oh *(in response to the stage lights dimming)*.

*Another spotlight appears on Young Luke with some other boys around his age. There's a flute player following the boys. On the backstage wall there appears a projection of a picture of a wealthy neighborhood and next to it a projection of a picture of an impoverished neighborhood.*

Narrator: There's young Luke, age eight. He was living in an affluent neighborhood in Kansas City, Missouri, when his mother was on sick leave from her government job.
 *The boys are walking and talking, and they come to a homeless drunk man.* Look at that. The boys just went from their wealthy neighborhood into the poor neighborhood of the city. (*points to the projection on the back wall*) It's as if the border between the poor section of the city and the wealthy section is almost nonexistent. Like the neighborhoods just blend together. Too bad we can't live like that in life, erase those imaginary boundaries we create between us.

*Some of the boys start throwing rocks at the homeless drunk man who is sleeping against some bags.*

Young boys: "Look at the old bum," "He's a waste," "Go get a job." *Young Luke also picks up rocks and throws them quietly but not directly at the man.*

Narrator: Either he's a bad aim, or he did that on purpose.

*The spotlights fade out on Young Luke and the boys. The flute player fades away. The stage lights come back to the present scene with Luke standing near Mr. Blunt's desk.*

Mr. Blunt: Luke Matthews?

*Luke quickly refocuses from his flashback.*

Luke: Yes, Mr. Blunt?

Mr. Blunt: Roy Blunt, but call me Roy. We have to use the Mr. and Ms. around here, some kinda throwback to the old welfare times of FDR. Everyone loves FDR. Go figure. Anyway, back here it's Roy.

*Roy Blunt comes around his desk to shake hands. Luke and Roy exchange handshakes, and Roy offers Luke a chair. Luke turns on his recording computer tablet. Roy Blunt sits back at his desk. Characters freeze in scene while the narrator speaks.*

Narrator: (is *standing near the desk)* Mr. Blunt was full of passion and idealism in his twenties. But he's sixty now. He looks worn down. The system will do it to you.

*Characters continue in the scene.*

Mr. Blunt: Is my staff treating you well?

Luke: (*stark, emotionless*) Sure, no problems. Thanks.

Mr. Blunt: (*pauses and gets a notification on his phone and then makes a disappointed face*) Luke, I hate to run out on you, but I have a meeting. Can we touch base another time?

Luke: Ah, yeah, sure. I understand. I'll be back in a few days.

Mr. Blunt: Great. I look forward to it. (*takes his coat and bag and walks with Luke towards the green glass doors.*)

Luke: (*looks down at the staff list from Claire*) Where's Dr. Markus?

Mr. Blunt: Right there. *Points to a desk with a medical stretcher near it.*

Narrator: First Jane Bidding, now Mr. Blunt. Are they really too busy to talk? What do these administrators do?

*Luke approaches Mr. Mark's desk.*

Narrator: Dr. James Markus, age thirty-two. James was outraged by the neglect of medical services for the poor, so he went into the unpopular specialty of primary care medicine. Yup a PCP. No one goes into primary care these days. There's no money in it, and you're really overworked.

Luke: Hello, Dr. Markus. Luke Matthews from *Times Today*. (*extending his hand*)

James: (*receives handshake*) Hi, James Markus. Nice to meet you. This is Mike, my assistant. (*exchange of hands between Mike and Luke*).

(*Characters freeze in scene.*)

Narrator: Mike, age twenty. Lives at home. No future career goals. His parents don't get involved in his life. His mother is a stay-at-home mom. His father has been a city worker his whole life. Society would think Mike was a failure, not climbing the ladder to success. (*pause*) But what defines success anyway?

Luke: Dr. Markus—

James: (*interrupts Luke*) Call me James. The agency makes me go by Dr. Mark with the clients.

Luke: *(nods)* Ok. Do you know why I'm here?

James: Yes, Claire told me. Sit down. What would you like to know?

*Phone rings. Mike picks up, speaks, and disconnects.*

Mike: James, Pearl said to come up front.

James: Sorry, Luke, I have to go out front. You're welcome to follow me.

Luke: Sure.

*James and Luke come through the green glass doors. Luke sits down in the waiting area and seems uncomfortable with all the children surrounding him.*

Pearl: *Pearl motions to Mrs. Baxter to come up, and there is an exchange of greetings between the two.* The database says she's medically cleared, but there's no medical report in the system.

James: Which doctor cleared her?

Pearl: Dr. Parks.

James: Let me give them a call. *(turns to Mrs. Baxter)* Don't worry, Mrs. Baxter. I'll take care of it.

*James starts talking on a phone.*
*Pearl glances at Luke sitting among the commotion of the children and then at James.*
*Mrs. Baxter starts to talk to Pearl and distracts her from looking at James.*

Mrs. Baxter: Nice young lady like yourself must have a nice husband.

Pearl: *(smiles)* No.

Mrs. Baxter: My husband died ten years ago. It's been so hard since he died. I'm eighty. I can't get a job. I just don't know what's gonna happen to me. *(pause)* And this is all so embarrassing. *(pause, tearful)*

*Luke approaches and interrupts Pearl as she is consoling Mrs. Baxter.*

Luke: *(socially acceptable smile)* Excuse me, Pearl, please tell Claire I'll be back tomorrow. Nice to meet you both. Goodnight.

Pearl: *(passively annoyed at being interrupted)* Yeah, sure, goodnight. *(turns back to Mrs. Baxter)*

*Luke waves goodbye to James, still on the phone. Luke is gathering up his bags in the waiting area.*

Pearl: *(consoling Mrs. Baxter)* It's going to be OK Mrs. Baxter. Mr. Ryan is working on things for you.

*Mrs. Baxter puts head down and slightly smiles.*
*Pearl finishes talking with Mrs. Baxter and has her sit in the waiting area. As Luke exits the front doors, Claire comes through the green glass doors.*

Claire: *(to Pearl)* Almost finished?
Pearl: *(timid and doesn't look at Claire)* Yes. Luke left. He'll be back tomorrow.

Claire: (*ignores Pearl's comment*) Last van comes at 5:03 p.m. going to Macy's Department Housing Placement. Then we close up.

*Claire goes back through the green glass doors and doesn't wait for Pearl to reply.*
*There is a call for van numbers from offstage, clients exit through the front doors and go off stage.*
*Pearl walks Mrs. Baxter to the front doors and gives her a hug and she exits the stage with other clients.*

*The welfare office employees start leaving through the front doors, and then Pearl leaves.*
*The narrator follows Pearl as she walks on the empty stage as if walking home.*
*On the back stage wall a projection of an early evening sky appears.*

Narrator: Pearl passes from a world of office lights to a dimly lit sky. (*points to sky*) The background noise of honking cars and headlights surrounds Pearl as if she has entered a new world. (*Lights appear on stage, car horns are heard*) The dark evening sky of late autumn is calling out to the approaching winter. (*in a whisper-loud voice*) Death is coming. (*Narrator opens his arms to the sky and throws his head back.*) The beauty of the colorful fall is ending, and the barren deadness of winter is creeping in with a beauty all its own.
*Narrator slowly pulls his head up and notices that Pearl is walking away, and he turns to follow her off stage.*

*Pearl re- enters stage and a flute player follows her playing music as Pearl approaches a simple set with a sofa and a table with one chair. She tosses herself on the sofa. The flute music fades away as a voice can be heard from Pearl's phone, the voice of her father talking about her younger brother losing his job and planning a twenty-first birthday party to cheer him up.*

Pearl: *(sighs out loud to herself in mocking tone)* Another beer fest where everyone is drunk but no one has a problem with alcohol.

Narrator: Pearl's father and her grandfather and several generations worked in union-run factories and warehouses. Over the years, many of the unions collapsed. Pearl's father and brothers scrambled for available jobs. Pearl was the only sibling of her family to go to college, an associate's degree. Pearl has always dreamed about returning to college someday. Money is hard to find for education these days.

*The stage lights dim except for a spotlight on Pearl and the narrator. Another spotlight appears in the corner of the stage on Young Pearl. The flute music starts up again and is faintly playing in the background.*

Narrator: Oh, Pearl, age five.

*Pearl's father is talking to Young Pearl, age five, and her three siblings. Pearl's father is holding a newborn baby in his arms.*

Pearl's father: Mom's in a beautiful place now. She's in heaven, and she's happy. Look at your little brother. *(smiles at the baby in his arms)* He's a gift from your mother.

*Pearl's father leans down and shows the children the baby as they crowd around.*

Narrator: Pearl didn't know the whole story of her mother's death; her father never spoke of it. But she remembers one of her brothers said her mother's age was a factor. She was forty-one. Pearl's father is still unable to speak about her mother's loss to this day. Pearl's youngest brother was spoiled by her father. He was afraid the boy would feel bad that his mother died in childbirth with him.

*Light fades on child Pearl, and all stage lights return to Pearl in her set.*

*Pearl sighs out loud. Pearl calls with her device and says, "Hi, Dad." Stage lights fade to black. Flute music stops.*

## Act 1, scene 2: October: Welfare Intake Office Q, a few days later

*Stage lights up.*
*Claire leans out of the green glass door and scans the room.*
Claire: Pearl?

*Pearl is squatting on the side of the copier.*

Pearl: Yes? I'm fixing the copier. It's broken again.

Narrator: Funny, with all the technology advancements, they still use this old fax copier. Broken and jammed fax copiers are an icon in welfare and social services. The copiers are always jammed by one employee and left for another employee to fix. And then when clients don't get the housing placement they wanted, welfare services blames the jammed fax copier. I know, sounds farfetched, right? It's actually happened. A lot.

Claire: Here's the welfare placement list. Looks like a lot of clients. Numbers will be high.
*Claire drops the list on the staff counter and disappears behind the green glass doors.*

*A few seconds later, Jane comes through the green glass doors.*

Jane: Pearl, did Claire give you the list? I need it.

*Pearl hands the list to Jane.*

Narrator: At community fundraisers, Jane is known as an advocate for the poor. (*raises his eyebrows*)

What does she do here? Typical welfare, tons of supervisors with titles and no one really knows what they do. (*pauses*) (*sarcastically*) But they are important, can't do without all those supervisors.

*Jane walks back through the green glass doors.*

*It's almost 9:00 a.m., and a few people are standing, and peering in the front doors. Mr. Blunt arrives and unlocks the doors. He waits patiently and holds the front doors. After the last person enters, Mr. Blunt walks in and over to the staff area.*

Mr. Blunt: Good morning, Pearl. Ready for another busy day?

Pearl: Sure Mr. Blunt. How're you?

Mr. Blunt: Good, thanks. Pearl, have yourself a good day.

*Mr. Blunt walks through the green glass doors. Pearl watches him walk away.*

Narrator: Pearl's dreams that Mr. Blunt would be a mentor faded soon after she started working here. Mr. Blunt is rarely at the office, and he doesn't return phone messages. (*pauses*) Yet, Pearl continues to believe her first impression of Mr. Blunt—that he genuinely cares about social justice for the poor.

*While Pearl is watching Mr. Blunt, Pearl does not see that Luke has entered through the front doors and has approached her.*

Luke: (*very dry and reserved*) Good morning, Pearl.

Pearl: (*turns when she hears her name*) Oh, yes, hi.

*There is silence for a few seconds.*

Luke: My research is done after I visit the Macy's site. The director and interviewer will start filming then. Have you ever been on camera before?

Pearl: Me? *(says firmly)* No. Why? Am I going to be interviewed?

Luke: You're the first contact that people have when they arrive here.

Pearl: Well, yes, but I would think you would focus on administrators.

Luke: I suggested that the interviewer take the public through the application process, as if they were applying for services.

Pearl: Oh. *(silence for few seconds)* Have you done a lot of research for documentaries?

Luke: Nope. I was just hired by the *Times Today* for this assignment. My first big break.

*A young woman and two small children approach the staff counter. Pearl smiles firmly at Luke and directs her attention toward the family.*

Luke: *(taking Pearl's nonverbal cue)* OK, I get it.

*Luke sits down and observes Pearl and takes notes on the role she plays with the family. He seems curious about her determination as well as puzzled at the same time.*

Claire: *(puts her head out of green glass doors and says to Luke)* Good, you're here. You need to review and sign confidentiality agreements. Everyone on your project needs to sign them. Come with me. I will give you the website to go on.

*Luke nods and follows Claire through the green glass doors. As Luke goes through the green glass doors, he looks back as the front doors open. Ronald P. Johnson in his late thirties, enters, looking disheveled and intoxicated on alcohol. He approaches Pearl and starts talking to her. He speaks loudly and is acting overly friendly to Pearl. Pearl sees that he can't fill out the forms, and calls James and tells him "A SA code".*
*Pearl tells Ronald Johnson to have a seat in the waiting area.*

*Luke approaches Pearl after he comes back through the green glass doors.*

Luke: (*in a frank tone*) Looks like he had a fun time last night.

*Pearl gives Luke a blank stare.*

Pearl: (*spoken quietly but sarcastic at Luke*) Sure if that's how you want to look at it.

*Luke clues into Pearl's seriousness. Pearl ignores Luke.*
*Pearl waves to Ronald to approach the staff counter.*

Ronald: Hello, young lady. By the way, did I ask how you are today?

Pearl: (*smiles warmly*) Yes, you did. I'm fine, thanks.

Ronald P. Johnson: (*sweetly*) Is it my turn now? What're you going to do with me Miss?

Pearl: Dr. Mark will give you a physical and send you over to the Macy's site. The nurse practitioner will keep an eye on you and give you some medications for the withdrawal. If you're sober you can stay there, ok?

Ronald: *(ignores Pearl and points to his chest forcefully)* Now, Miss, do you know who I am? I'm Ronald P. Johnson. I'm a member of the Johnson family. You know what our family is famous for? I know I don't have to tell you, right? You know my family name. Well, I know we lost everything. But that's what happens in a consumer culture if you don't want to change. I told my family they needed to roll with the changes. Didn't listen. *He starts dancing with a rolling motion.*

*James comes out of the green glass doors and politely interrupts the man.*

James: Good morning, everyone. *(to the waiting room)* Hello, sir. What's your name?

Ronald: Ronald P. Johnson. *(with anger)* I need some respect here, don't you recognize me? I—

James: *(calm manner)* Sorry, excuse me, Mr. Johnson. *(turns to Pearl)* Let's wait on Mr. Johnson's forms till later when he feels better. *James takes the man with him through the green glass doors.*

Ronald: *(less angry)* Well, like I said, my family—yup they made it, they had the American Dream… *The green glass doors shut.*

Narrator: Pearl won't hear what made this man's family famous. In this day, many people's stories were real—embellished a little, but real.

*Stage lights down.*
*Stage lights up.*

*Narrator moves the manual clock to 2pm.*
*The scene moves behind the green glass doors to James's desk.*
*Luke is at James's desk engaged in conversation with James and*
*Mike. Ronald Johnson is lying down on a stretcher.*

James: Medical services is me and Mike. (*points to Mike and gives him a thumbs up*) My assistant and medical van driver.

Luke: So, what does this medical clinic do?

James: Well, we're a PCP office and ER in one. The welfare clients are not allowed to go the ER or hospital unless I send them. And we also have to make sure all the clients have medical clearance for welfare housing placement sites. A couple years ago, we had some medical epidemics at a couple of the housing sites, so now everyone has to have a medical clearance before placement.

Luke: (*pauses and reads some notes*) Weren't these clinics created to stop people from misusing hospital ERs?

James: Yup, they were. Medicaid couldn't pay the costs from the ERs. (*pauses a few seconds*) Hey, do you remember the commercials when healthcare and Dunkin Donuts united?

Luke: (*controlled smile*) Sure. I was a kid. I always got a donut after a sick visit.

James: Yeah, well, those corporate coffee businesses paid for most of the start-up costs and rent for these welfare medical clinics. Starbucks still covers most of the rent for our clinic.

Luke: So, anyone without private insurance can come here?

James: Yeah, pretty much. But the new welfare system wants people to have a *documented work history* to get medical services. Of course, I sometimes look the other way, if you know what I mean.

Luke: (*Nods and looks at his list of questions*) So does this new medical system work?

James: No. I believe it compromises lives; but the government statistics are still inconclusive. (*rolls his eyes and makes a mocking face*)

Luke: How so?

James: We're not equipped to handle a lot of emergency situations, and lives are lost having to send people here first. Oh, and, forget about preventative care. No time for it.

*Ronald Johnson sits up on the stretcher in the corner, he has sobered up some.*

James: Feeling better Mr. Johnson? (*he sits up and comes off the stretcher*) Come sit down. Is it ok if Mr. Luke listens? He's doing a documentary on the new welfare system.

Ronald: Call me Ron doc. Of course, of course. I have nothing to hide. Nothing left to hide. (*hangs his head down*).

Luke: (*stoic smile*) Thanks.

Ronald: So, Doc, can I get that free housing? I heard I can get free housing with the right brain scan?

James: (*pats Ronald on the shoulder in a comforting way and also looks at Luke*) Ah, Brain Scans. For years, there was a big battle with mental health providers and the government. The government could no longer afford to give SSI payments for mental health disabilities. Congress had to agree on something. The new science technology swayed Congress's final decision: brain scans. There's your brain Ron. *(points to standing screen)*

Ronald: Well look at that. A beauty, eh? But, will it get me some free housing, doc?

James: *(laughs and smiles)* A beauty for sure. *(gets serious)* But, unfortunately no free housing.

Luke: *(interrupts and disconnected)* What does free housing mean?

James: It waives the work requirement.

Luke: What kinda brain scans get free housing?

James: Brain scans that show a *likelihood* of schizophrenia, bipolar, or depression qualify for free housing and services. *(points to the screen)* Brain scans, that seem to point to, ah, say personality disorders, PTSD, or anxiety, take years to qualify for free housing and services. Look. There are two brain scans that qualify for free housing, and there's your brain scan, Ron. *(points to the screen)* *(makes a mocking face)* How they came up with allowing some people free services or not is beyond me. And, they won't even consider substance abuse issues. Stupid medical model dictates everything in America.

Ronald: So, my brain isn't sick enough? *(pause)* I wanted the free housing where I just have to volunteer. *(pauses and looks down and ashamed)* I can't figure out why I can't get myself together. I'm a screw up I guess. *(pauses)* Just like my mother always said. *(pause)*

I use to be able to hide behind my family fortune. *(pause)* But that's gone. And no one in my family wants to help me now.

*Luke is looking at Ronald not sure how to react to his statement.*

James: *(compassionately)* Ron, your brain is stuck from all the alcohol, and it's misleading you. But there's nothing wrong with you; your brain can be healthy again. Give it time. The government should help your brain to get better. I'm sorry you don't qualify.

Ronald: *(puts his head down and looks at the floor)* A stuck brain you say?

James: Ron; your brain has *you* hostage. But you can free it. I see the person *you* are and you're a good person. Don't forget that. You have the answers to get better. Keep looking.

Ronald: *(still discouraged but a little brighter)* Well if you say so doc.

*Silence for a few seconds.*

Luke: *(flatly)* What do you mean Ron about volunteering?

Ronald: Oh, I don't know; someone told me that (*looks at James*).

James: If you qualify for free housing, you have to volunteer 5 hours a week at your housing placement. Oh, but if you're "severely mentally disabled" they can exempt you.

*Mr. Blunt approaches James's desk, and they all greet each other.*

Mr. Blunt: *(to Luke)* I have a bit of time to talk now. Does this work for you?

Luke: Sure.

*Luke ends the conversation and walks to Mr. Blunt's desk and sit down. Narrator follows them.*

Mr. Blunt: So, how can I be of assistance?

Luke: Well, I'd like your perspective on this new welfare system.

Mr. Blunt: *(speaks passionately)* I've been working in welfare for almost forty years. I watched the old welfare system crash and the new system emerge. This welfare system will have its time, and it'll change. I'm retiring before the next meltdown. Don't have the energy. Damn bureaucratic rules just drain you. Waste time and waste money. And, you know, idealistic me, I believed that people change the system for the betterment of others. *(bitter laugh)* Nope. When money gets tight, everyone starts asking, "Why should I work and pay for your food and shelter?"

Luke: *(disconnected)* I see.

Mr. Blunt: Now, if you don't have resources or money, how do you get to advance in our society? How do you pull out of poverty? Do we really want everyone to succeed? That could threaten our comfort and security. We say, "Oh, the poor children," but do we really want all the poor families to have everything that we do?

Luke: Do you believe some people are truly victims of poverty and unable to escape that poverty?

Mr. Blunt: Do you think poor children dream that they will be in desperate and poor situations when they grow up? Heck, no. But what do they have to look forward to or dream about when they look around and see the *hopelessness* around them? (*pause*) Will they ever learn to believe there is another life out there when poverty is all they know? *Mr. Blunt looks at his phone, gets up and starts putting his coat on.* Sorry, I have to get to a meeting.

Luke: (*stands up*) Well, thanks for your insight, Mr. Blunt.

Mr. Blunt: *(reaches out his hand to shake Luke's hand, and Luke receives handshake)* It's wonderful to have you here. Any more questions, call me. I look forward to seeing the end result.

*Luke heads through the green glass doors to the waiting area. In the background a spot light appears on Mr. Bob Parker standing outside the welfare front doors, in his usual spot giving a speech. Luke goes out the front doors to listen.*

Mr. Bob Parker: Let's talk mental health. Now, there are categories for mental health, and only some people have *real* mental health conditions. Can you believe this is where science took us? Classifying mental health as *serious* or *non-serious*. How can we label only some human suffering as acceptable? (*pauses*) *Oh, and,* if the *serious* mentally ill do not comply with medication recommendations, they can be discharged from their free housing. Yeah, it's true. Believe it! It has happened. (*pauses*) This is what you get when you have uneducated, immoral politicians leading the country. I saw it all coming to this; but nobody wanted to listen to a ranting homeless man!

*A person walks by and puts money in Mr. Parker's hat.*

*Stage lights down.*

## Act 1, scene 3: November: Macy's Department Store Welfare Placement, a few days later

*Stage lights up.*

*Bob Parker outside the set of the department store placement, giving a speech with his hat out in front of him, lights focused on him.*

Bob Parker: Consumerism. A necessary evil of our capitalist society? I guess. But it's consuming us, it's chewing us up and spitting us out. And what's left? Emptiness. Yes, Emptiness. (*voice fades away as focus moves to department store set*)

*Stage Lights focus on the department store set. There is a big sign hanging down that reads Macy's.*
*The set consists of simple gray chairs scattered around the stage and two sets of bunk beds, and a desk for the Nurse Practitioner. There is a table with a few thin computer monitors. Signs hanging on stage say, "Bathroom" "Thrift store" "Cafeteria"*

Narrator: Every couple of months, Pearl visits the Macy's Department Store Housing site. These visits are required by the government to report that the residents have been "checked in" with. (*points to an old sign that reads Macy's*). Macy's. What a regal store in its day. You were definitely someone if you shopped at Macy's.

*Pearl sits down to jot down her contact notes on her computer tablet, when Luke comes over.*

Luke: (*direct and without emotions*) So tell me more about these sites.

Pearl: (*looks up*) The federal government gave out grants to states so they would purchase these vacant department stores and create communal living programs. Remember, these places all went vacant with the boom of online stores. Rather odd they never changed the names. But, there was such an urgency for housing, I guess they never had time, nor the money. They needed something quick.

Luke: Ah, I remember. So, the communal living programs now provide all the welfare services in one, right? The government ended Medicaid cards, food stamps, and cash and rent assistance?

Pearl: Yup. Systemized everything to an extreme. Now the housing comes with food, medical care, transportation, and daycare. Choices were eliminated. This department store houses over a hundred beds cramped into office cubicles. There's a common bathroom and a cafeteria here, as well as thrift stores for clothing and personal hygiene items.

Luke: *(points to set of two bunk beds)* There's not much privacy in those cubicles.

Pearl: Nope. The government is criticized a lot for it. But I don't see anyone donating money to improve the situation.

*Luke looks down and is typing, so Pearl continues with what she is doing; a few seconds of silence.*

Luke: *(pauses for a few moments and looks around the main area)* I assumed people in need of housing were unemployed with no skills. These are working, middle-class families.

Pearl: Yeah, these cubicles are home for many working, middle-class families. *(in a bitter tone)* The American dream. The land of opportunity. It's a myth.

Luke: (*makes a dismissive/uncertain face at Pearl's last statement and doesn't respond to it*)
Ronald Johnson said I could talk with him in his cubicle.

*Pearl appears frustrated with Luke's dismissiveness. Luke walks away from Pearl. Pearl continues recording her contact notes but watches Luke with curiosity. The two men greet each other. Luke barely fits a chair into the cubicle. Mr. Johnson is sitting on his top bunk bed.*

Luke: *Luke continues to direct questions at Mr. Johnson; he is very methodical and disconnected, looking down at his own notes often.* Now, how do you move out of this housing placement?

Ronald: I need a steady job to get those fancy boarding houses and apartments.

Luke: What are boarding houses like?

Ronald: Well, you get your own room. There's a community kitchen, and you can do your own cooking. Here it's cafeteria style everyday. I feel like I'm a kid in school.

Luke: How do you get your own apartment?

Ronald: If you're successful in a boarding house and there's an opening, you can graduate to your own apartment. But it's hard to do. I don't see that happening for me.

Luke: (*pauses and glances at his tablet and is quietly studying something*) And there are medical services over there? (*points to nurse practitioner in the distance*)

Ronald:  Yeah, nurse practitioners, the NP's. They give you the basic stuff. Great if you're not real sick. (*pause*) My roommate in this bunk bed has a broken foot. He said it's been five weeks and he still hasn't gotten to see a specialist.   Everything needs an approval; it's all so slow.

Luke: OK. (*pauses and scans his tablet*) And what about transportation in this new welfare system?

Ronald: (*points offstage*) See those vans and cars over there? They take people to work and outside medical appointments.

Luke: (*looks down at his notes and reads*) I read that the new car and van system saves money and also generates more tax money.

Ronald: It probably does. People can't make excuses that they can't work because they don't have a ride. (*pause*) And, you know, in the old days, those Medicaid cabs were making a fortune. Had an old friend that owned a cab company and he made a ton of money in the day of Medicaid cabs.

*Ronald looks over near the nurse practitioner area. There is light sign that shows the number 50.*

Ronald: (*looks at a ticket in his hand*) My number is up. I need to get my medicine.

Luke: How long does a person usually wait to see an NP?

Ronald: I took this number about two hours ago. I've seen people wait up to four hours.

Luke: Oh. (*uncomfortable*)

*They walk to the nurse practitioner desk. Luke introduces himself.*

Luke: Are there enough medicines for everyone?

Nurse Practitioner: Well, we always have the mass-produced drugs, but sometimes a drug helps one person and not another. Unfortunately, you have to try the available drugs, and if one of those doesn't help, you end up getting sicker before you can get a different one. And it's very hard to get different drugs. Excuse me. I have to get back to work.

Luke: *(looking down at his notes)* Yes, thanks for your time. (*Nurse practitioner smiles.*)
(*puts out his hand to Ronald with a slight smile*) Thanks Ron. I might have you interviewed for the film. Would that be OK?

Ronald: (*returns the handshake*) Sure. Whatever you need. I'm an open book.

Lukes: *smiles slightly and nods.*

*Pearl approaches Luke and tells him she needs to leave. Luke nods but asks a question.*

Luke: What are those for? (*points to rows of monitors on tables nearby*)

Pearl: They're job databases. Mr. Blunt is in charge of keeping up relationships with the area employers. You know, no one who lives here can work here? (*Luke looks questioningly at Pearl.*) There are jobs they can't even fill here, like security, daycare workers, van drivers, but they won't change the policy. So, everything is always short staffed at these sites.

Luke: Well, they must have a good reason for the policy?

*Pearl makes a dismissive face at Luke, which Luke ignores. There is silence between them.*
*Luke walks away to pack up his bag. A boy approaches Luke. Pearl listens with curiosity.*

Anthony: Hi. My name's Anthony. What's yours?

Luke: Luke.

*Luke is finishing his notes while talking to the boy, and Luke seems distracted and uninterested in the boy.*

Anthony: (*in a bold, childish voice*) What are you doing here?

Luke: (*distracted and looking at notes, very emotionless*) Taking notes for a film.

Anthony: A film?

Luke: A film about where you live.

Anthony: Why?

Luke: Well, I want other people to see how you live, and maybe this'll help you get a better place to live.

Anthony: What's wrong with this place?

*Luke stops writing and looks at the boy.*

Luke: (*stammers a bit*) Well, I mean there's nothing wrong with this place.

Anthony: It's a great place to live. All my friends are here. And there's always food. Sometimes it's not great, but it's warm.

Luke: Ok.

Anthony: You're going to tell them in your film that this is a great place to live, right?

Luke: I'll keep that in mind. But what about your parents? Wouldn't they like a bigger place to live?

Anthony: Well, I don't know about them. I haven't seen them in years. I live here with my older brother. I'm scared of the dark, so I don't know if I want a bigger place than my cubie. My brother is right below me if I need him.

Luke: (*briefly smiles and faintly laughs at the boy, out of character for Luke*) Ah. Thanks for your input, young man. You have given me a different view of your home.

Anthony: Can I tell my friends that I'll be in your film?

Luke: You can tell them you gave me some ideas for my film. How about that?

Anthony: Thanks, Luke. (*puts his hand out to shake Luke's hand*)

Luke: (*receives the handshake*) Thank you, Anthony.

*Anthony walks away, and Luke watches him and appears lost in thought after this conversation with this little boy.*

Narrator: The profound insight of a child. He knows what makes him happy in life.

*Luke packs up his bag, Pearl joins him, and they exit the stage. Stage lights down.*

## Act 2, scene 1: January: Documentary prescreening dinner

*The staff from Welfare Intake Office Q and* Times Today *staff at a prescreening dinner party. A set with a few circular tables and chairs. There is a coat checking table.*

Narrator: January. The first snow of the year. *(points at a projection on the back wall of a picture of a window showing snowy trees).* Look at the trees outlined in snow. The fluffy snow hides the course, barren bark of the empty trees. (*very dramatic expression*) The warm air temperature is threatening to melt the snow away and reveal the empty, dark branches. But, the snow seems to be clinging to the branches, trying to keep the beautiful picture alive. Ah, so much like life. We only want to see the beautiful picture, right? Not the ugly barren.

*Narrator grabs a drink and an appetizer from a nearby wait staff, and moves close to where Luke is standing and talking to the director of the documentary and a sponsor. Music is playing in the background.*

Director of Documentary: Luke, you did a fine job. *(talking to Luke then turns to the sponsor he is talking to)* I couldn't have done it without him. He did all the research. I just had to piece it together.

Narrator: Luke is enjoying the attention he's getting from the director, even if the director is pitching the documentary to a sponsor. Yes, Luke, conquer! *(pause)* Oh, there's Pearl.

*Luke is momentarily distracted from his conversation as he watches Pearl enter and go stand by herself in the corner; he seems to be studying her.*

Director of Documentary: Great talking with you. *The sponsor leaves, and the director quickly pulls Luke over to another sponsor.* Luke, I have someone else I want you to meet.

*James also sees Pearl enter and appears to be lost in thought while gazing at her.*

Narrator: (*nods toward James*) Earlier today at the intake office, James was rather abrupt with Pearl when she tried to discuss her concerns about Claire. James wants to practice medicine. He doesn't want to be bothered with staff problems.

*James approaches Pearl in the dining room. James waves at waiter for another glass of wine.*

James: Hi, Pearl. That's a nice dress. Pretty colors.

Pearl: (*smiles*) Thanks. Looks like a nice turnout. (*pauses and some silence*) It'll be interesting to watch us in the film.

James: (*nods yes*)

Speaker: Good evening. Please take your seats.

*James and Pearl head to a table.*

Narrator: Well, look at Roy Blunt. He's certainly enjoying the spotlight. That's what big administers love, the spotlight.
*Roy Blunt is among network executives and film sponsors, talking and smiling.*

Speaker: Good evening everyone. We are grateful that we have people committed to the service of others. (*pause*) This film was made to shed light on the social justice issues that are ignored in our country, to give a voice to the people who have no way to speak up for themselves. (*pause*) Ok let's begin the film.

*The film starts on the backstage wall. Stage lights fade to black. Stage lights up.*
*The film and dinner are over; the people are getting their coats and exiting the stage.*

Luke: Pearl?

Pearl: (*turns around*) Hi, Luke. I liked it.

Luke: (*reserved but curious*) You liked it?

Pearl: Yeah. I liked the details, and it was accurate.
(*James approaches them.*)

James: Hey Luke! I loved it. (*puts his hand out to shake Luke's hand*) Great dinner too.

Luke: Thanks. (*with a flat tone*) I'm glad you both liked it.

*The manager is asking everyone to continue to exit; the studio is closing.*

James: Guess we need to get moving. Pearl, you need a ride home?

Pearl: Yeah, thanks. Let me get my coat. *Pearl walks to get her coat.*

James: Luke, will you come to our after-work dinner chats? Ah, and sometimes we do a weekend afternoon trip.

Luke: Sure. I'll tell Ryan to keep me posted.

*Pearl is approaching with her coat.*

James: OK, see you around then. *(They shake hands.)* Pearl, I'll bring the car around.

Pearl: Door-to-door pickup sounds great. *(smiling)*

*James exits the stage. Pearl is putting her coat on, and the button catches her dress.*

Luke: *(reaches toward Pearl in a very attentive manner that is new for Luke)* Let me help you.

Pearl: *(surprised by Luke's attention)* Oh, I'm fine. Just stuck for a moment. *(Luke steps back, more reserved and nods.)*

Luke: I look forward to still seeing everyone.

Pearl: Ok.  Oh, I see James out there. *(looks offstage)* Ok. Bye. *(Luke smiles with reserved emotion).*

*Pearl turns, looks over her shoulder, and smiles hesitantly at Luke as she exits the stage.*
*Stage lights down.*

## Act 2, scene 2: February: Welfare Intake Office Q, a dreary Friday

*The staff enter the front doors, and rhythmically stomp and shake the snowy slush onto the carpet by the front door. The snow is imaginary. Bob Parker is outside the front doors, holding his hat in his hands and speaking to those entering. We can't hear what he is saying.*
*All that is heard is the stomping of feet in rhythm as people enter the front doors.*

Narrator: Listen to that sound. *(silence for several seconds to hear the rhythm of stomping)* The damp air of February is clinging to the staff as they enter the building. The snow is dirty and murky, the end of winter is approaching.

*The stomping stops. Narrator sits in the waiting room chair with his guitar and starts playing softly. Margaret Brown is peeking in the front doors. She finally decides to enter. Supervisor Jane Bidding enters behind her.*

Jane: Excuse me. *(friendly and professional but anxious)* Can I help you? The doors aren't open for the public yet.

*Margaret appears to be weary and is speaking with slow speech; she is in her mid-twenties. Her clothing is tidy but shabby; she is underdressed for the winter weather.*

Margaret: Ah, ma'am, I'm i-ill. Please *(pause)* c-c-can I see the doctor? I need to sit down.

Jane: *(friendly)* Well, we're not open yet. *(looking at the clock on the wall)* Oh, well, look at that. It's eight fifty-nine. *(in a overly nice but patronizing tone)* OK, sit down, but you have to wait. I don't know if the doctor is here yet, and you have to register. Pearl will be out any minute.

*Pearl comes out of the green glass doors into the waiting area.*
 Oh, here she is! (*Jane excitedly approaches Pearl.*) Pearl, I need to speak to you. (*She turns back to Margaret and acts as if she cares*) What's your name?

Margaret: Margaret Brown. (*Her head is nodding toward the ground, eyes half closing; she has a very pale, sunken look on her face.*)

Jane: (*says privately to Pearl and overly instructional*) This woman says she needs a doctor. Register her and see if she has a history here. I think this might be…well, you know. (*Jane's voice trails to a whisper, and Jane is mumbling something*)

Pearl: (*annoyed tone at Jane*) What?

Jane: (*trying to maintain friendly professionalism seeming a little bit inpatient*) Pearl, call Dr. Mark, OK? I need to go. And I can't stay late tonight. I've been putting in extra time lately. (*pauses and returns to professional compassionate tone*) Ms. Brown, Pearl will get you started. All set Pearl?

Pearl: Yes, Jane. (*Pearl doesn't look at Jane she is on the phone with James.*)
 *We see Pearl very attentive and concerned and helping Margaret. Jane makes a flustered, helpless look and passes through the green glass doors.*

Jane: (*reappears back in waiting area*) OK, Pearl, all done with this woman? Please make sure that she is taken care of. Unfortunately, I need to get to the homeless coalition committee breakfast. *Jane smiles at Margaret.*

Pearl: (*with quiet frustration*) Yes.
*Pearl avoids looking at Jane as Jane heads toward the front doors to leave.*

*Jane looks back at Pearl and makes a exasperated face because Pearl is ignoring her.*

Narrator: (*makes a confused face*) What does Jane Bidding do again? I never see her in her office. Oh right, she attends all the homeless county meetings. Sits around a table and talks for hours about how to save the poor. She makes up all the ideas to help these people. She's popular as an advocate for the poor. (*mockingly*) How could I forget that?

*James enters the waiting area from the green glass doors. Pearl is sitting next to Margaret, holding her arm as she sits in the chair.*

James: Pearl?

Pearl: Margaret, this is Dr. Mark. (*to James*) Call an ER Van?

James:( *nods yes*) Mike is on his way back, but I don't want to risk waiting.

*Pearl returns to the staff area, to call an ER van.*
*Margaret nods her head slightly at Pearl and goes with James through the green glass doors. She is stumbling a bit and leaning against James, and James speaks to her.*

James: *(to Margaret)* Tell me what you took recently.

Margaret: I -I think it was stronger than usual or not the same (*pauses due to not feeling well*) I was trying to to…stop, but I just can't. I know my family (*voice mumbles and trails off*) I don't know how I became like this. I don't want to do this. (*tearful*) Don't they understand? I'm not trying to hurt them…(*voice trails off*)

James: (*nods and listens*) It's ok Margaret. You're sick. Tell me what you think you used.

Margret: (*holding back more tears*) I used a few bags of heroin. But it never hits me like, like this.
*Margret puts her head down, tears flowing from her eyes. The green glass doors close behind James and Margaret.*

*The waiting area is still empty. Pearl's phone rings. She picks up.*

Ryan: *(calling Pearl's phone)* Hey, can you check a few names for me?

Pearl: Sure.

*Ryan repeats a few names to Pearl. Pearl repeats names back with some dates.*

Ryan: James is trying to get a dinner together for later. You in?

Pearl: Ah, I don't know.

Ryan: Come on. I can stay for dinner this time. No wedding planning with Marie. She's going out with some friends. And Luke's coming.

Pearl: Well, if you're staying for dinner, I guess I have to come. It's rare you don't have wedding planning with Marie. *(smiles while talking)*

Ryan: Great. See you after work. *(disconnects)*

*Stage light comes on James desk area/stretcher.*

Margaret: I'm feeling spasms in my hands and arms. *(looking at her hands and arms, crying, suddenly, falls off the chair to the floor)*
James: *(puts her on nearby stretcher)* Margaret!

Margaret: *(unconscious and is having a seizure)*

*James raises his voice and can be heard desperately talking and pleading to Margaret as he's medically attending to her. James hits emergency button, a beeping noise comes on Pearl's phone in the staff area. Pearl runs through the green glass doors.*

James: Margaret, stay with me.

*Margaret's body is convulsing.*

James: Margaret, stay with me. Margaret? Margaret!

*Pearl is standing motionless. Margaret's body suddenly becomes motionless.*

James: *(grabs wrist to check vitals)* Damn it. *(throws his hands up in frustration)*

*James and Pearl stand in silence, and then Pearl puts her head down, tears in her eyes and turns and heads back through the green glass doors.*

*There is silence in the office except for the narrator in the corner of the waiting room playing the guitar to a couple of children dancing in the waiting room. Narrator is slowly strumming the song ([ "If I*

*Had a Hammer Ruthie Foster blues version"]). A client in the waiting room stands up and starts singing the song.*

*The stage lights start to dim on everyone except the narrator, the client singing and children in the waiting room. The sounds of the emergency van can be heard in the distance as the song is coming to an end. As the emergency sounds get closer, they get louder and overpower the narrator and client's song until we only hear the loud emergency sounds. Stage lights down, and there's only the flashing lights of the emergency van until they fade away.*

*Stage lights up.*

*Narrator approaches a manual clock on the wall and moves the clock hands from 9:00 a.m. to 2:00 p.m.*
*Pearl and James are in the staff area; the waiting room is almost empty.*

James: Quiet in here. *(silence between them)* Thanks for your help earlier. (*Pearl nods her head. There is silence for several seconds.)* You OK?

Pearl: *(looks down and doesn't make eye contact)* Just have to accept it. Right? Isn't that what we have to keep doing? Just accept it, nothing to be done? Can't fight the system, nope too powerful.

James: (*quietly looks down*)

*Silence between them. Both are just standing in the staff area, looking exhausted and staring out into the waiting room.*

James: Did Ryan call about dinner?

Pearl: *(says with a melancholy tone)* Yeah, I said I would go.

James: OK, well then, I'll see you later. (*turns to leave and smiles at Pearl in a comforting way*)

*Pearl responds by smiling affectionately back at James. James momentarily places his hand on her shoulder as a supportive gesture. James turns and heads for the green glass doors, and then Pearl continues reading. James glances back at Pearl with compassion as he walks through the green glass doors.*

Narrator: The day continued, and the day ended. (*moves the hands of the clock to 4:55 p.m.*) The outside doors are ready to be locked. Oh, here comes the advocate for the poor.

Jane: (*bubbly but anxious and exaggerated expressions*) Pearl, what time is it? (*turns to look at the clock, doesn't wait for Pearl to respond*) Oh, not quite five. I thought it was six, and I was going to ask why the doors were still open. (*Pearl is studying her laptop; Jane keeps talking.*) Well, what a day! So stressful. All these meetings, and arguments, and conflicts. It never ends. Everyone thinks their ideas are going to save lives and end poverty. Pearl? Are you listening to me?

Pearl: (*with an annoyed tone*) Yes, Jane. I'm waiting for Claire to finish the stats so I can enter them.

Jane: OK, I'll go see where Claire is. *She goes through the green glass doors.*

*The green glass doors open, and Claire exits.*

Claire: (*hands some papers to Pearl and is reading something else*) Goodnight, have a good one.

Pearl: You too. (*Pearl quickly glances at the papers from Claire and timidly speaks.*) Wait, Claire, I…I think the stats are wrong. I…I didn't see these people today.

Claire: Those are from the other state workers.

Pearl: OK. (*in a timid voice*) I thought…Joanne was out sick today?

Claire: You're overthinking this. I'll check it tomorrow. You don't need to be working this late. It's five after five. Go on now. Get going. (*Claire laughs in a bit of a mocking way and smiles and goes through the green glass doors.*)

*Mike exits the green glass doors and heads towards the front doors.*

Mike: Hey, Pearl, heading over to Hatfields?

Pearl: Yeah. Be there shortly. (*Pearl smiles.*)

(*Mike smiles and exits through the doors.*)

Narrator: The weekend is here.

*People start exiting through the front doors. The front doors open and shut in rhythm, and that is all that can be heard for a few moments.*

Pearl: (*talking out loud to herself*) Yes, a few extra names on the list as usual.

*Jane enters from the green glass doors.*

Jane: OK, Pearl, you have a great night.

Pearl: You too. (*smiles curtly*)
*Keyboard on stage and narrator is playing instrumental song.*
*Mr. Bob Parker has appeared outside the front doors in his usual*
*spot. Jane quickly smiles at him and keeps going.*

*Pearl goes through the green glass doors and comes back through*
*with her coat and bag and goes through the front doors. Narrator*
*stops keyboard and follows after Pearl. Pearl smiles at Bob Parker,*
*and he nods. Pearl exits the stage.*
*Narrator shakes hands with Bob Parker and follows after Pearl*
*offstage.*

*Stage lights down.*

*Stage lights up, and Pearl approaches a projection of a picture of a*
*large brick building on the backstage wall. Narrator follows behind*
*Pearl.*

Narrator: This was an old factory warehouse that was renovated to a
restaurant years ago (*looks at the building.*) A beautiful brick
building with large windows and high ceilings (*points to the people*
*sitting at tables, eating dinner.*) For years now, many diners have
enjoyed themselves, feasted, and drank in this building. (*pause*) A
century ago, this building employed factory workers who were
underpaid, and overworked, and probably hungry. How history can
change.

*Pearl enters a simple set with a few dinner tables and chairs. Pearl*
*greets the work group: James, Mike, Luke, and Ryan. James pulls a*
*chair up for Pearl to join them.*

Ryan: Pearl, I was just talking wedding plans. This wedding thing is
so stressful. Marie and I are really getting to know each other better
by picking out wedding cakes. (*laughs*) Lots of bickering. We

recently realized we need to stay focused on the reason we decided to get married.

Pearl: Sounds a bit stressful.

Ryan: Yeah, hey, but we decided on a date. Only a little bickering over that. (*laughs*) August thirty-first. You're all invited.

Pearl: Oh, that's nice.

*Waiter takes dinner orders. There is some music playing in the background.*

James: (*to waiter*) Another round please. (*pause*) Pearl, any idealistic and positive viewpoints today? (*in a lighthearted, teasing manner*)

Pearl: Oh, I'm tired. (*teases back*) No energy for optimism today. (*smiles*)

James: Ah, too bad.

Pearl: Well, James, you could share a quote from your father. Something like "the world is full of manipulating, lying people, and we will never eliminate jealousy, violence, and deception." (*smiles and laughs*)

James: (*teases back*) I could, Pearl. Smash everyone with some realism. (*laughs*)

(*Quiet for a moment*)

James: Luke, when's the documentary being released?

Luke: The target date is in April.

James: Great. What are you working on now?

Luke: Promotion work. But I start my new assignment soon: American garbage.

James: Now *that's* a topic that needs some light shed on it.

Pearl: The amount of e-waste that has accumulated over the years is incredible.

Mike: My dad is an administrator at the city garbage site. There's a gridlock with what to do about the growing garbage problem.

Luke: I'm interviewing three scientists who work on government grants at some of the most troubling garbage dumps in the county. I've never been to a garbage dump.

Mike: I went all the time as a kid.

*Dinner is served, James asks for another alcoholic drink. Three singers come out and sing a song. [song O, America Celtic Women]. The three singers are characters from the play: Margret Brown and two older children. The singing continues, and Pearl and her group exit the dining set and can be seen talking. Luke, James, and Pearl start heading toward a sign that says Downtown Bus. Ryan and Mike say good-bye and exit the stage.*

James: Oh, I'm on call starting at seven a.m. I have to stop at the hospital and pick up a computer tablet. *James starts to exit the stage and speaks loudly to Pearl.* Pearl, plan a day trip this weekend with everyone. I'm off call Sunday at noon.

Pearl: No promises.

James: You always say that. *He smiles as he exits the stage.*

Narrator: The streetlight is flickering. *(points to the light)* The temperature has gotten colder. *(zips his jacket)* The damp, cold air of February is still around us.

*A projection of a picture of a bus appears on the back wall, and there are a few seats onstage set to represent the bus seats. There are single posters hanging around on the white boards. Pearl and Luke sit down. Narrator follows them. There is silence for a few seconds, and then the engine of the bus is heard as it speeds up.*

Luke: *(points to a poster print)* Did you see that art show at the 72nd gallery?

Pearl: Yes! I loved that featured painting, *Crowded Main Street* *(pointing to the poster print of an artistic abstract picture of a main street with abandoned storefronts and lots of different people walking on the main street)*.

Luke: *(flatly)* It had nice colors.

Pearl: *(speaks with excitement about the print on the poster and dismisses Luke)* It was more than just nice colors. The closed storefronts intrigued me. What kind of business were they? How did the owners feel when they lost their shops? And the people on the streets all have blank looks on their faces, yet there's such emotion in those blank, serious faces.

Luke: *(in a reserved and dismissive way)* What? *(pause)* Emotion in a blank, serious face? *(controlled laugh and smiles)* OK. It just seems like a crowded main street with closed storefronts. I took their faces to be abstract technique, no?

Pearl: (*talks as if almost ignoring Luke's comments and continues talking about the painting*) We don't know who these people are. Maybe they're important; maybe they're not. (*points to a spot on the poster*) I belong there. Everyone is an individual, but no one person is more important than another. There, my importance wouldn't matter. There'd be no one to impress with stories of success.

*Luke seems intrigued by Pearl's observations but also baffled. He stands up, getting ready to get off the bus.*

Luke: Ah, well, that's an interesting view. No expectations. (*Luke smiles hesitantly; he seems confused and taken aback by Pearl's excitement. Pearl glances at Luke and looks confused by his comment.*)
(*Luke exiting*) Always a pleasure, Pearl. (*smiles warmly this time at Pearl as if he can't help it despite his reserved nature*) Let me know if you plan a day trip Sunday, OK?

Pearl: (*smiles, still distracted by the poster and her thoughts*) Sure, see you soon. Goodnight. (*smiles*)

*Pearls curiously watches Luke as he exits. She appears to be studying him as he fades away. She is not sure what to think of him but there is something that keeps her watching him. Then, Pearl turns and glances at the people on the bus.*

Narrator: (*gestures at the people*) What are the lives of these people like? Anyone important here?

*Stage lights fade to black*

***Act 3, scene 1: March: Welfare Intake Office Q, a Friday, a day of awakening***
*Stage lights up.*
*Narrator outside the front doors welfare office.*

Narrator: Spring is fighting to get rid of winter. The spring sun is trying to warm the chilly March winds.
*Narrator zips his jacket. Pearl enters stage, and enters the front doors. The city landscapers are working outside the front doors, pretending to clean up.*

Narrator: Flower beds are being cleaned out, and leftover fall leaves are being blown into bags. You can smell the fresh earth *(narrator smells the air)* as it's turned up by the gardeners raking the soil. And today is Pearl's meeting with Mr. Blunt. Yes, Pearl is meeting with Mr. Blunt. A new beginning perhaps? Spring always offers a new beginning.

*Narrator walks in the front doors. State workers arrive for work. Pearl is in the staff area. The waiting room fills up with people, and the daily work begins.*

Narrator: Well, the morning went fast. Oh, look: already eleven a.m. *(manually moves the clock with his hands to 11:00am)*

Pearl: *(on phone)* OK, Mr. Blunt, you won't be in until early afternoon. A breakfast meeting with landlords. Sure, I'll tell Jane. *Pearl disconnects and says to herself out loud—no one is around her.* Guess you forgot about our meeting. *Pearl beeps Jane.* Jane? *(we only hear Pearl talking to Jane)* Mr. Blunt will not be in until early afternoon; he said he has a breakfast meeting with landlords. *(Pearl disconnects.)*

*Waiting area has people coming and going.*

Narrator: Oh, wow. *(looks at the clock and moves the clock hands)* It's one p.m. already.

*Glass doors open; James enters waiting area.*

James: Pearl?

Pearl: Hi. *(slightly smiles at James.)*

James: *(with enthusiasm)* Hey, what are you up to?

Pearl: Just reading. *Pearl appears preoccupied.*

James: Did you see Luke on the news? That "Garbage in America" clip?

Pearl: Yeah, sounds interesting.

James: Ryan told me. You know me; I never catch the news much.

*There is silence, and James sees that Pearl appears distracted and makes a face at her.*

Pearl: Sorry, James, I'm not in a talkative mood today.

James: OK, I'll leave you to reading. *(glances to see what she is reading)* New Welfare requirements? I can't compete with those.

Pearl: *James makes her smile, and she teases him.* It's more interesting than your chatter.

James: Ah, so be it then. *(laughs)*

*Pearl's mood is a little lighter now. James looks back at her as he goes through the glass doors; he seems to have a look as if taken with her. Mary the intern passes him as they go through the doors together. Mary the intern goes to the staff waiting area.*

Mary: Hi, Pearl.

Pearl: Hi, Mary. How are you?

Mary: Good, thanks. What are you reading?

Pearl: New welfare requirements. By the time you read them, they change again. *(laughs) (Mary laughs.)* More new forms and rules. Ugh.

Mary: There is just so much to learn and figure out.

*In the waiting area is a young mother with two children, ages two and one. She appears frazzled and short on patience and almost in tears trying to finish the forms.*

Mary: *(looks at young mother)* Must be hard. But at least she'll get some help for herself and the children, right?

Pearl: I guess. But ever since our country has fallen on hard times, this system has been squeezed dry of humanity and concern for others. *(pauses)* I don't know. Maybe it was always like this. *(with passion and frustration)* But how does that young mother get a start? She has no education, no work history, no housing history, no family support. She has a family history that spans three generations of welfare services. Will she escape?
*Pearl goes to help and comfort the mother.*

*Narrator is looking outside the front doors. Rita Ballington enters through the front doors; she is quietly tearful and slurring her words. Claire is walking with Rita Ballington and speaking harshly toward her. As Claire and Rita enter the waiting room, a small crowd of people starts gathering around.*

Claire: *(abruptly and nasty tone)* OK, all of you go sit down or head outside. Pearl?!

Rita: I don't feel well. *(leaning forward and holding her head)*

Claire: Yes, I can see that. Not enough pills left to take away the pain today?

*Rita starts to stagger around; she falls to the floor. The chair breaks her fall. Pearl rushes toward the woman, but Claire puts her hand up at Pearl.*

Claire: This woman is high; let her sleep it off. I'll call SA transport. Leave her.
*Claire turns around and goes through the green glass doors.*

Pearl: *(ignores Claire and goes to Rita)* Can I get you anything? A pillow? What is your name? *(Pearl helps her prop her head onto the chair.)*

Rita: Ye— *(She puts her head down on chair and closes her eyes.)*

Pearl: Mary, go to Dr. Mark's office and get a pillow and blanket. He's at rounds but should be coming soon.

*Pearl is next to Rita comforting her. Mary exits and then returns with items.*

*Mary and Pearl lift her body to lie across the chairs. Pearl notices that Rita has an injury on her forehead. They move back behind the staff area to talk. Pearl calls for a transport.*

Narrator: *(looks at Rita lying on the chairs)* Maybe mid-fifties. Her clothes are clean, rather expensive and stylish.

Pearl: I hope James gets back before the SA transport arrives.

Mary: Why?

Pearl: The SA transport team comes in a van, so this woman will have to sit in a van seat with a seatbelt. She will be taken to a SA clinic where she could wait hours. *(pause)*
People under the influence of substances are not allowed to seek ambulance services to the hospital emergency rooms unless sent by a doctor.

*(Silence for a few seconds)*

Mary: That supervisor was unfriendly. What was her name again? I keep mixing up all these supervisors.

Pearl: Claire. *(pauses)* Her anger and judgment is mean. Addiction is a human thing. Everyone just looks at the weakness of addicted people, when addiction rears its ugly side. Don't we all have an ugly side? No one wants to see that addicted people have strengths and gifts too, they are human. They're some of the most perceptive and artistic people I have ever met.

*Pearl and Mary are distracted by loud yelling from outside the front doors. Bob Parker, disheveled in appearance, opens one of the front doors and starts yelling in.*

Bob Parker: *(appears intoxicated)* What good do you do? You don't help people. You just make them more helpless. You just make yourself think you are doing good for the less fortunate. It's a scam. A government scam. The system is in place to make the do-gooders feel better about their happy lives, to make them enjoy their meals more and feel less guilty. Social services, ahh…blah, it's garbage. How does it make me feel? Dependent. Dependent on a system that spits out different rules to me every time I try to escape the system. *(spits on the ground)* What's America about? It's about individualism, take care of your own, race to that top, and find the American dream. But then what? Sit on the dream and be vigilant. Why? Because you might lose the dream. Yes, the American dream might be snatched away.

*Bob Parker spits on the ground again, throws his hands up in the air, and shakes his head. The front door closes when he throws his hands up. The doors reopen when security appears, and one door is propped open. There is an exchange of words with Bob Parker and security. Security guards start casually chatting with Bob Parker as if they know him.*

Bob Parker: Ah, fellows, what's wrong with a little political debate? Isn't that what America is all about?
*A new voice is heard approaching from off stage.*

Narrator: A familiar voice.

*Mr. Blunt approaches.*

Mr. Blunt: What's going on, Mr. Parker?

*Mr. Blunt shakes Bob Parker's hand, brief exchange of words. Pearl and Mary are watching.*

Narrator: The two men look about the same age. They could have been in school together. Perhaps. But these two men followed different paths in life.

*Mr. Blunt starts to go through the front doors, and Bob Parker runs to his bag and gives Mr. Blunt a paper from his bag. They say good-byes.*

*Mr. Blunt enters the waiting area and walks past Rita Ballington and doesn't notice her at first. Mr. Blunt is still looking out the front doors at Bob Parker. As he turns back around, he then notices her lying on the chairs.*

Mr. Blunt: Pearl, is this woman OK?

Pearl: Not really. *(Pearl lifts her head toward the front doors as the SA team enters.)* But SA is here. I didn't want to move her since she has an injury.

*SA transport team enters and starts tending to the woman, taking her vitals.*

Mr. Blunt: I'll be in my office if anyone needs me.

*As he is opening the green glass doors, Pearl calls his name and he turns around.*

Pearl: Mr. Blunt, we had an appointment this morning?

Mr. Blunt: *(thinks for a minute)* Oh, Pearl, yes. I'm sorry. I must have forgotten to put it on my calendar. Seems to happen a lot lately. Come back when you're done for the day, OK?

Pearl: All right.

*Rita Ballington is sitting up, and the transport team is trying to talk with her. James comes in the front doors and starts asking questions.*

James: I think this woman needs to go to the hospital. Get the stretcher, please.
*James gets her on the stretcher and takes her through the green glass doors. SA transport team follows James.*
James: *(leans back out the green glass doors)* How long has she been here?

Pearl: About twenty minutes. Claire insisted that I call SA transport. I'm glad you arrived; Claire was rude to her.

James: Looks like she has a significant head injury.

*Rita Ballington is resting/sleeping comfortably on the stretcher near James desk. James goes over to a mobile computer scanner and gently presses the woman's fingertips on the scanner. James lays her hand back down and waits for the computer to search. A white bottle cap falls out of her blazer. He sees the bottle hanging out of her blazer pocket. He takes the empty bottle from her blazer pocket and he puts it with the cap near her on the stretcher.*

*The computer reads out loud, "Rita Ballington, age forty-eight, no outstanding medical issues, married, no homeless record."*

*The SA Tech stirs Rita to take her blood. James takes the opportunity to talk to her.*

James: Hi, Rita Ballington. Can you tell me how many you took of these?

Rita: Ahh, I don't know—a few. I went for a drive, and I couldn't stop feeling nervous, so I pulled over and took a few. I parked the car and then went to get a coffee. I don't remember anything else. Where am I?

James: You're at the Welfare Intake Office Q. I think you took too many of these and you passed out. Looks like you hit your head. You have some symptoms of a concussion. You'll need some stitches.

Rita: Did you call my husband?

James: Not yet. Just got your information.

Rita: Oh, my pocketbook and ID—I don't know where they are. My phone is gone. Let me call my husband.

James: Sure. I'll call an ambulance. I assume you have private insurance?

Rita: Yes, my husband will bring the information. Where are you sending me?

James: To the Center Hospital ER.

Rita: OK. Thank you.
*She can be heard talking to her husband.*
*James starts looking at his computer.*

Narrator: A word on James. His father was from an affluent, upper-class family that touted a few generations of surgeons. His mother's family's wealth came from the original empires of pharmaceutical companies. His parents' families often socialized together when his parents were in their youth, and the families were quite pleased when James's parents married. Oh.

*The stage goes dark except for a spotlight on James and the narrator.*

I'm getting used to the dark stage.

*There is a light that slowly appears in the corner of the stage, and there is Young James with his mother and nanny. James' mother is in a bed and appears to be sleeping. There is a cello player who plays in the scene.*

Narrator: There's six-year-old James.

Nanny: Your mother is tired and needs to rest.

Young James: *(says it in an angry tone)* I just want to go rest with my mother! *He sees some empty prescription bottles on the ground; he studies them for several seconds, and he picks them up and throws them.* That's all she needs. She needs more medicine to get better.

*He storms offstage, the nanny watches him leave. The cello plays for 15 seconds, and music fades away.*

*Stage light dims on Young James, and stage lights reappear in the present scene.*

Rita: Excuse me, Doctor? Doctor?

James: *(distracted briefly by his thoughts of the flashback)* Yes?

Rita: My husband is asking if he should meet me at the hospital. When will I be transferred?

James: Tell your husband you should be there within a half hour.

*Rita disconnects with her husband. She is groggy still.*

James: What do you think you were nervous about? When you took those xanax?

Rita: Well, I'm a nervous person; I always have been. *(pauses unsure if she wants to say more).*
I need to maintain my appearance you know, *(makes a serious face)* so everyone sees I have it all together. It's a lot of pressure. *(defensive)* I need the medication.

*James nods as he listens. Silence for few seconds.*

Rita: Life seems so empty some days *(looks away with a distant emotionless look).*

*James gives a consoling look to Rita. The ambulance crew interrupt them as they come through the green glass doors. They prepare and take Rita.*
*James goes to the waiting area with Pearl, and they watch the ambulance crew and SA team head out the front doors.*

James: Once your addicted, you might as well have psychosis. You can't make good decisions. Why don't people want to see this?

Pearl: *(sighs)* I don't know. That stupid War on Drugs campaign has crippled America for decades. Nothing but stigma and judgement came out of that movement.

James: *(turns toward Pearl with conviction)* There's a war going on alright, but it's inside America. No one believes it though. Nope. Everyone just blames the addict who buys the drugs. But the drug addict isn't the enemy we need to fight. The drug dealer isn't the enemy either. Can't win a war if you don't want to see who the real enemy is.

Pearl: Yup.

James: Can't fight what we don't want to see. The enemy is inside all of us. If we all looked closely we'd see that addiction lies in all of us. We wouldn't judge the drug addict so harshly if we smashed the truth in our own faces.

Pearl: Yeah. And it's tearing apart American families; the war is eroding America from the inside.

James: Yup. American families are casualties of this war. *(mocking)* War on Drugs. *(silence for few seconds)* I'll go talk to Blunt about Claire.

Pearl: *(rather surprised)* Oh, OK.

*James heads through the green glass doors toward Mr. Blunt's desk. James pretends to knock and approaches Mr. Blunt.*

James: Roy, I need a moment.

Mr. Blunt: Yes, James, sit down. *(Mr. Blunt takes off his glasses.)*

James: Roy, you need to talk to Claire. Pearl said she was rude to that woman in the waiting room.

Mr. Blunt: Really? The one that was high? Pearl said SA was on the way?

James: She had a head injury. And by the way, that woman was Barry Ballington's wife. She wasn't here for our services; she just wandered in. But I don't care who that woman is. Claire shouldn't treat anyone like that.

Mr. Blunt: Oh, Barry Ballington, who owns all those new energy plants?

James: Yes, but did you hear what I said about Claire?

Mr. Blunt: OK, James, I'll talk to her. This isn't like her; she must have been busy. Hey, how was that conference you attended about that new drug for treating substance abuse?

James: *(waves his arms in an exaggerated motion)* Well, it's being touted as the cure for substance abuse. It's backed by some genetic research funded by pharmaceutical companies. I'm not impressed. And why must we treat substance abuse as if we have to cure it or vaccinate it? *James turns and leaves.*

*Stage lights dim, and stage lights back on to waiting area. Pearl is talking to Mary in the staff area. They are watching the families pick up the toys in the waiting ares, and they start to head offstage to the vans.*

Pearl: How do you ask a parent to sit and play with their children when they're worried where they're going and how they'll provide for their children?

*The waiting room empties out; it is quiet. Narrator moves clock to 5:05 p.m.*

Narrator: Gotta keep the time; this old manual clock needs to keep ticking.

Mary: *(has her coat and is heading out the front doors)* Thanks Pearl. See you tomorrow.

Pearl: Sure, good night.
*Pearl goes through the green glass doors, to Blunt's desk and pretends to knock.*

Mr. Blunt: Come in.
*He motions to Pearl to sit down; he is on a headset. Mr. Blunt's voice is causal.*

Narrator: *(looks around)* Rather dark back here. *(looks at a small picture on the corner of desk.)* A picture of Blunt's wife and daughter. *Pearl is also looking at the picture on Blunt's desk.* He's separated from his wife, perhaps divorced at this point.

*Blunt finishes his conversation and takes off his headset.*

Mr. Blunt: *(writing and doesn't look up)* Hi Pearl. Sorry it's rather dark back here.

Pearl: *(smiles)* Hi. Yeah, a little.

Mr. Blunt: *(pauses while he writes some notes)* Well Pearl, what can I help you with?

*Pearl is looking down at her hands and wringing them in her lap. Pearl looks up from her hands and directly at Roy Blunt. Narrator picks up his guitar and starts to slightly strum it.*

Pearl: Well, I…I wanted to speak with you. About Claire.

Mr. Blunt: Alright. *(gestures as if to say "continue")*

Pearl: *(says with firmness but voice quivering a bit)* The daily stats are sometimes off. The totals are wrong.

Mr. Blunt: Really? Um, Ok. Do we need to send Claire back to elementary school and teach her to add? *(Mr. Blunt laughs.)*

Pearl: *(fake smile)* Sometimes, there are client names that repeat on the monthly stats. Clients who never returned for services.

Mr. Blunt: *(more serious tone)* Are you implying something?

Pearl: *(speaking less confidently and more softly)* Well, I'm not sure. The client names stay on the daily stats, and then they're marked off as successfully discharged at the end of the month.

Mr. Blunt: All of these clients never returned?

Pearl: *(stammering)* Well, I...I don't know. I only looked up a few.

Mr. Blunt: Why are you looking at discharge dispositions? That's not part of your job.

Pearl: *(voice starts cracking and speaks softly)* I...I just didn't know what to do with the names.

Mr. Blunt: So why tell me now? Or why not tell Jane?

Pearl: I don't know. *(pause)* I did hear one of the managers joking with Claire about getting bonuses for successful discharges.

Mr. Blunt: Supervisors don't get bonuses for successful discharges. *(pauses)* They only receive bonuses if they show they're cutting costs. *Roy gets up and starts pacing anxiously behind his desk.* Pearl, do you know what it's like to work in social services for almost forty years? You're young. You've just started your career. When I was your age, I was idealistic too. I thought everyone should work together and make a better world. But you know where my idealism took me? Nowhere. It didn't get more services for the poor. It did nothing. *(pauses)* So I took a high position that would give me the power to make changes. Are there problems in our agency? Sure, maybe. But you have to accept this is just how things are. There are problems everywhere.

*Pearl's eyes are staring at the floor. The narrator is raising his eyes in response to Roy's lecture to Pearl.*

Mr. Blunt: What do you want me to do? Talk to Claire?

Pearl: *(starts to stand up to get out of chair, and her voice is quivering and emotional)* Sure, Roy, whatever you want to do with the information is up to you.

Mr. Blunt: OK, Pearl, I need to finish up. Have a good weekend. *He gives her a smile in a dismissive way. Pearl faintly smiles and leaves the office.*

Narrator: Typical administrator, shoot the messenger. This is why change never happens. *Narrator puts guitar against wall.*

*Pearl gathers up her coat and bag and heads out of the green glass doors. She pushes open the front doors, and a wind hits her in the face. Narrator follows behind her.*

Narrator: Ah, I feel a fresh, breezy wind. Feels like the air of spring. *Narrator puts his head into the wind to enjoy the breeze but then is distracted by Pearl walking away.* Wow, she's walking fast.

*The stage is empty. Suddenly a man comes from off stage and is walking next to Pearl. He is dressed in a suit that is neat and clean but worn. He follows Pearl and approaches her with a pamphlet.*

Narrator: It's typical at this time of day to see missionaries of the churches walking around the city and recruiting members. The rush-hour time is popular to reach the people and increase membership. Churches are eager to increase membership.

Church Man: You're a fast walker, young lady.

*Pearl smiles and slows down but continues walking.*

Church Man: Miss, take this pamphlet? Read it. Give it a chance. *He gently moves the pamphlet toward her.*

Pearl: OK. *She takes the handout and keeps walking.*

Church Man: *(stops walking and yells after her)* Any questions, come to our church. Address is at the bottom. And good evening to you, miss!

*Pearl is about to place the handout in her pocket without reading it, but as she goes to do this, something on the handout catches her eye. She stops and reads the pamphlet.*

Pearl: *(speaking out loud to herself, frustrated):* "Love your neighbor." Love your neighbor. How? I feel pressure to beat out my neighbor.

Narrator: America has been grounded in the myth of individualism over the past centuries. Beat someone out for the best land or for the best job. Do whatever you need to get to the top. Even cheat a little.

Succeed, succeed, succeed. It does rather conflict with the idea of loving your neighbor.

Pearl: How about listen to your neighbor? I'm in an entry-level position in a government agency, and no one will listen to me. No one will listen to me; I'm too idealistic.

Narrator: Now that's interesting. Listen to your neighbor. I like it. You don't have to make the commitment of loving them, just listening to them. Huh.

*Pearl enters her apartment set, tosses herself on the couch, and throws a pillow over her face.*
*Stage lights to black.*

**Act 3, scene 2: April: a Saturday morning, a museum**

*Stage lights come on.*
*There is a projection of a city museum and garden on the back stage wall. A simple set of two small tables with chairs is on stage. There is a sign hanging from the ceiling: "Museum Exhibit: The Downfall: Welfare at the End of the Twentieth Century."*
*Pearl is sitting at one of the tables reading.*

Narrator: *(points to museum projection)* Look at those trees, full of white spring blossoms. So fluffy and soft and serene against the graffitied brick buildings. They almost look fake. Oh, look it's Luke.
*Luke approaches Pearl.*

Luke: Pearl?

*Pearl looks up from her book.*

Pearl: Oh, Luke, hi.

Luke: How're things?

Pearl: Fine, thanks. What about you?

*Bob Parker appears outside the coffee shop tables; he starts talking and puts his hat on the ground for tips.*

Luke: No complaints. *(points at Bob Parker)* I remember seeing him around the welfare intake office. I see him around the city alot.

Pearl: Yeah, he use to use welfare services years ago. I've never seen him come in our intake office. He often hangs outside the front doors, or wanders around the city.

Luke: He always looks like he's making speeches.

Pearl: He is making speeches. And if you stop and listen, he's quite profound some days.

Luke: *(rather dismissive with disbelief)* Really?

*Luke leans over to listen. Suddenly we hear Bob Parker.*

Bob Parker: High school is often where you seal your fate. There are two kinds of kids in high school: you got your conformer and you got your rebel. The conformer kid studies hard, joins all the school clubs, sports, and races to be successful, to reach the American dream. *(waves his arms about)* The rebel kid trys to reach the dream a different way; he just can't stomach the race to nowhere. So the rebel kid takes some risks and doesn't follow the rules. Which kid sees more truth? Yes, I said which kid sees the truth about life? No, not the conformer, the rebel, of course *(laughs heartily)* *(Someone puts money in his hat.)* Thank you, sir. The problem is once you choose a rebel role, America doesn't let you go back to the conformer role. Nope, can't switch. Cause you get *(with fearful and harsh voice)* branded! Yup. You're tarnished goods. So, what's the lesson here folks? If you can stomach the conformer role, take it. Hey, having a few drinks can help you cope. Live by FOMA! *(yells out)* Fear of missing out!

*A woman is heard calling Luke's name, and Luke turns away from the speech.*

Luke: Lauren, over here. (*Luke waves at the woman.*)

*Lauren is very striking looking and appears to be confident in her mannerism. She approaches Luke.*

Luke: Lauren, I want to introduce you to a friend of mine. This is Pearl; she was in the documentary on the new welfare system. *Pearl and Lauren smile at each other and say hi.*

Lauren: Nice to meet you. I hate to run off, but I'm starved. I'm going to get in line. *(smiles politely)*

Luke: OK, sure, I'll be right there.

*Lauren leaves them. Luke and Pearl are left in silence.*

Luke: *(points to Bob Parker and with reservation and doubt says)* I don't know what he's talking about. The rebel kid is more truthful? Who's a rebel?

Pearl: *(defensive, ignores Luke's comments)* I find him intelligent.

*Silence. Both appear to not agree with the other. Luke says something socially acceptable to break the tension.*

Luke: So are you seeing the show?

Pearl: Yeah, as soon as my friend gets here. She's running late, as usual.
*Silence.*
Luke: How's everyone: Bob, James, Ryan?

Pearl: Good. Busy. *(silence)* We have to get another dinner together. *(silence)* Oh, I forgot. James told me you got a new position with that documentary team?

Luke: Yeah, a one-year position with In Focus. The pressure is on.

Pearl: (*matter of fact*) Well, the research you did on our agency was good.

Luke: Thanks.

*A woman enters onstage and waves to Pearl. She approaches Pearl.*

Beatrice: Sorry I'm late! I don't know what excuse to give you except I just don't know how to be on time. *(She laughs a little.)* Oh, I'm sorry; I didn't mean to run in and interrupt your conversation.

Pearl: Oh, Beatrice, this is Luke Matthews. You remember the documentary I was in? Well, Luke did the research for it.

Beatrice: Oh, wonderful to finally meet you. I can't wait to see it. Pearl says it's superb. When is it released?

Luke: The end of April.

Beatrice: Well, I will have Pearl remind me so that I can watch it. How exciting.

*Pearl notices that Lauren is waving, trying to get Luke's attention.*

Pearl: I think your friend is waving to you.

Luke: *(turns to wave at Lauren)* Oh. Well, enjoy your day. Nice to meet you, Beatrice. Oh, Pearl, keep me in mind for a dinner. I'll be in town for the next few weeks, and then I'll be traveling.

Pearl: OK, sure. Take care. *(smiles)*

*Luke leaves.*

Beatrice: So, my friend, you still have patience for me even though I keep you waiting every time we get together?

Pearl: *(seems distracted, looking in the direction of Luke)* Do I have a choice? *(teasingly)*

Beatrice: Now I see you looking after that man with a mysterious look on your face. I remember you mentioning him before. But you didn't mention that he was so handsome. *(smiles playfully)*

Pearl: Well, handsome or not, I didn't find his personality so pleasing when I met him. Rather self-absorbed and uncompassionate.

Beatrice: And what do you find him to be now?

Pearl: I don't know. I don't quite understand him. He seems so unfeeling.

Beatrice: You spend a lot of time thinking about someone you say you don't care for.

Pearl: *(a little defensive)* You know me; I'm always interested in what makes people tick.

Beatrice: That's true. Since we're on the subject, has that attractive doctor asked you out on a date yet? I do believe that he's a match for you. What was his name?

Pearl: James? Why, no, Bea, we're just friends. I don't see that developing anytime soon. He is much too busy with his career. Now can we stop creating a love life for me? I'm done for now.

Beatrice: OK, but that was almost a year ago, Pearl. *(Beatrice sees Pearl's annoyed face.)* OK, on to another topic: my romance and my wedding plans! Roger and I are planning a date for next November. What do you think? The end of fall, the most barren of months. What better than to brighten it with love? All the beautiful leaves are bagged up, and the trees are stark and brown and gray. Am I romantic or what? Well, and the prices for wedding halls are much cheaper in November.

Narrator: *(sighs)* What a lot of energy and expectation for a one-day celebration.

*Narrator goes over to a nearby keyboard and starts playing a simple melody very softly.*
*Stage lights fade to the end of the music.*

*Stage lights up.*

*Pearl and Beatrice are near the museum sign.*
*Pearl and Beatrice are reading programs. Luke and Lauren walk arm in arm, and talk with another couple. Pearl can be seen peering over at Luke and his friends. There are scattered standing white boards on stage to represent screens to project pictures on.*

Narrator: To an observer, Luke and Lauren appear to well matched, both outgoing, commanding personalities, easy to socialize with. Both very attractive. The American dream couple.

Beatrice: Pearl? Where do you want to start? Pearl?

Pearl: *She quickly looks down at her program.* Um?

Beatrice: My, you are reading intently.

Pearl: *(ignores Beatrice's comment and points)* Let's go see the photos of the old welfare system from the nineties.

Beatrice: Sounds like a plan.

*Pearl and Beatrice approach the standing white boards set up like screens, circulating pictures representing the former welfare system in the 1990s. The pictures pause for about one minute each, and then the next picture comes on.*

Pearl: These photos of the New York City welfare employees are so interesting. There were so many employees back then. Look at this photo of the old welfare Medicaid card. Look at that SSI application. Oh, a picture of a crowded welfare waiting room, children playing on the waiting-room chairs and floor. Look at these children, posing right in the front of the camera with big smiles. The adults don't look so happy though.

Beatrice: *(says it in a rather bored tone)* Interesting, Pearl. Well, I am going to move on. Do you still want to study these?

Pearl: Yes, I'll catch up in a bit.

*Beatrice exits scene. Luke approaches Pearl.*

Luke: So, this interests you, eh?

Pearl: *(startled at first)* Uh, yeah.

Luke: These children look so happy in these photos. It's hard to believe they were in such desperate situations.

Pearl: *(a little defensive)* Children always have a way of seeing the wonder of the everyday, even when times are hard.

*A photo appears of a hospital emergency waiting room full of people. Pearl hits a button that has a loud audio automated voice that booms out in the audience/stage area. The automated voice has an authoritative commanding tone that's hard to ignore.*

Audio Automated Voice: In the twentieth century, many people with Medicaid went to the emergency room for minor things: ear infections, poison ivy, fevers, colds. These emergency-room visits were costly to the Medicaid system and, combined with the rise in healthcare costs, led to the bankruptcy of the old Medicaid system in the twenty-first century.

Pearl: The end of Medicaid began the end of choices for people in the welfare system.

Luke: *(starkly)* Well, people abused the choices. Centralizing medical services was a way to stop the abuse of the system.

Pearl: *(with emotion)* It's much easier to blame the poor people for taking advantage of the system and destroying Medicaid. But they didn't create the system. They just used what they were given.

Luke: Ahh. *(surprised at Pearl's response and not sure how to respond)*

Pearl: *(with emotion and conviction)* What about the failing US economy and government debt that could no longer pay for Medicaid and the old welfare system? The government that failed to monitor and amend the system so it didn't crash?

*Silence as the next slide appears, "1996 Welfare Reforms" and a photo of a blown-up welfare employment search record. Pearl quickly hits the audio button again.*

Luke: Well— *(interrupted by the audio automated voice)*

Audio Automated Voice: The 1996 Welfare Reforms expected people to work or show that they were trying to get work in order to receive welfare benefits. People had to document that they spent forty hours a week looking for jobs. Many people didn't have reliable daycare and transportation, so many people didn't end up working.

Pearl: *(looking at the welfare document)* Goodness, everything was paper back then.

Luke: Well, I was going to say— *(Pearl interrupts Luke by pushing the audio button again.)*

Audio Automated Voice: People who didn't want to deal with the 1996 welfare requirements took jobs off the books, leaving less tax revenue in the economy to pay for welfare services. Many people also turned to illegal ways of making money, including selling drugs.

Pearl: History can be so mythical. This is not true for everyone.

Luke: It must have some significant truth if they're noting it.

Pearl: *(very passionate and with expression)* History is often molded to highlight small truths. Molding history makes us feel better about our choices as a country, to justify our government's decisions.

Luke: *(shows some frustration but seems to be drawn into trying to follow Pearl's intensity)* At least there's a system that provides for the poor. The old system crashed because it was abused. People sold the food stamps for drugs, and drug dealers made millions off of SSI checks. I don't really understand your emotions about all this.

Pearl: *(silent for several seconds)* I don't understand your lack of emotions.

*Both are standing in silence, looking at the other samples of slides of welfare documents passing in front of them. The body language of both appears frustrated with each other.*

 Luke: Well, I'm going. *Luke turns to leave.*

Pearl: *(rather curt)* OK, sure.

*Luke exits. Pearl continues to stand, watching the slides for a second. Pearl looks at the time and exits.*
 *Stage lights fade to black.*

***Act 3, scene 3: May: Welfare Intake Office Q, a Monday morning, a day of encounters***

*Stage lights up.*

*Pearl opens the front doors; it is 9:00 a.m. A few families enter the building. Claire comes through the green glass doors with a welfare worker, Stella.*

Claire: Pearl?

Pearl: Yes?

Claire: *(very cold in her attitude to Pearl)* Stella will sit here for a few minutes. I need to speak to you.

*Claire turns and goes back through the green glass doors and doesn't wait for Pearl. Pearl finishes something on her laptop, closes it and slowly walks through the green glass doors. The narrator follows Pearl.*

Narrator: It's quiet here. No welfare workers dictating client demographics into their voice-activated devices. *Pearl is hesitating and looking timid as she looks ahead to Claire's desk.* Onward, Pearl. *Narrator points towards Claire, and Pearl follows as if she heard the narrator.* The uncommon silence in here is crushing Pearl as she knocks on Claire's office door. *Pearl pretends to knock on a door.*

Claire: *(curt voice)* Come in.
*Claire's voice is heard in conversation, and her fingers are moving on her laptop. She has a headset on, so we can only hear Claire talking. Claire's back is to Pearl. Claire continues talking. Pearl sits down.*

Claire: I like the new bangs on you. (*pause*) Yes, it looks different. What does Mary say? (*pause*) Well, it looks very stylish. Did you do your eyebrows too? (*pause*) I love the color. And the trim is right for your eyes, really makes them stand out. Where did you get the eyebrows done? (*pause*) Ah, good to know. Are you still going for the facials to help relax the wrinkles? (*pause*) I see. OK. Take care, sweetie. Talk soon.

Narrator: The years of social media took a toll on people, and the drive to be noticed, get attention, be popular and look young became a daily game to win. (*pauses*) Well, wait. I can't blame it all on social media. Guess it's always been like this; social media just made it easier to do. (*laughs*) AH, America is always looking for the answers out there, and not in here. (*points to his heart*).
(*looks at picture on Claire's desk*) I wonder who those kids are in the picture? I think she has some kids, and a niece or nephew she cares for, but no one really knows her whole story.

Claire: Pearl? (*with her back to Pearl*)

Pearl: Yes.

*Claire slowly turns her chair around. There is silence.*

Claire: Mr. Blunt tells me you have some concerns about the stats?

Pearl: So, you remember those numbers, um…that were wrong for families that were recorded as successfully p-placed?
*Pearl is fumbling with her words and is losing confidence when she speaks. Her shyness is apparent as she speaks softly, and there is a struggle to keep her voice from quivering.*

Claire: (*intimidating glance at Pearl*) How so?

Pearl: There…there have been times when numbers don't add up. Ah, for families discharged.

Claire: Really? I told Mr. Blunt I was quite confused about your assumption. All these long, tedious hours. Perhaps I must have added wrong? How conscientious of you to bring this to my attention. *(in a very forceful way)* I would never do anything like that intentionally. You know that, right?

Pearl: OK. *(pause)* Well, is that all? *Pearl is wringing her hands in her lap. Pearl starts to stand up, sensing Claire is disregarding her.*

Claire: *(silence for a few seconds and very patronizing)* You seem so dedicated. Do you like your job?

Pearl: *(says with seriousness and caution)* Yes.

Claire: Great. Keep those numbers up. That's how we stay open, you know. The old Medicaid days are over.

*Claire smiles smugly and turns her chair around so that she is no longer facing Pearl.*

Narrator: Now, did we really think that a quiet compassionate person like Pearl could take on a manipulative greedy supervisor like Claire, and win? Maybe in the movies; but not real life.

*Pearl timidly leaves Claire's, and heads toward the green glass doors. Narrator continues to follow her.*

Jane: Pearl? Pearl? *(calling anxiously and excitedly after Pearl from her desk)* Do you hear me, Pearl?

Pearl: *(suddenly hears Jane, turns around)* Ah, no, I didn't hear you. What did you need?

Jane: Please get out front. Stella is overwhelmed. I tried to help her, but I am much too busy myself.

Pearl: *(says softly, still seems frazzled from the talk with Claire. )*I'm headed there now.

Narrator: I wouldn't mind a supervisor job here. Not much to do except make other people work. Oh, except Jane works so hard to be an advocate for the poor. *(looks over her shoulder)*
She's ordering curtains for her house. Sure, important stuff.

*Pearl pushes open the green glass doors into the waiting area. There is a line of clients and Stella is looking frazzled. As soon as Pearl comes into the waiting room, Stella turns and leaves through the green glass doors.*

Narrator: Look at Stella; she's fleeing for the green glass doors. Safe behind the green glass doors. I see Mary the intern was trying to help. But like any intern, she's not really sure what to do.

*The waiting room is crowded.*

Pearl: *(to Mary the intern)* I constantly see familiar faces. What's keeping them from freeing themselves from this system? What holds them back, the system or themselves?

*A violin and a viola player appear on opposite sides of the stage and begin softly playing alternative pieces that are complementing but conflicting with each other. They play for about one minute while Pearl is interacting with clients.*

Narrator: The front doors open with a gust of wind that is stereotypical of a spring day. *(Bob Parker, with a cane, enters the front doors with the wind behind him. Pearl looks up; she recognizes him.)* It's Mr. Bob Parker. Oh, the cane is new. He's the one who makes a commotion in front of the building with his speeches about America. I guess he doesn't have any speeches today. He hasn't stepped inside this office in years.

*Bob Parker walks to the staff area, where Pearl is standing.*

Pearl: Hello, can I help you?

*He is quiet for a few seconds as if catching his breath.*

Bob Parker: *(with his head down and minimal eye contact)* Miss, I told myself I'd never come back here, ever. That was four years ago, before you were here. Now, I don't need your help with those nonsense welfare services. Nope. I can take care of myself these days. But I need to see your Dr. Mark. Have a few questions for him.

Pearl: Well, yeah, sure. I can give you—

*Bob Parker interrupts Pearl.*

Bob Parker: My mother raised me and my three brothers on welfare. I tried to escape miss, yes I did. But here I am at fifty-seven, a man who must face his worst fear. I never escaped. *(pause)*
As a child, I wanted to grow up and live the American dream. The American dream. *(pause)*
At twelve, I found beer and weed, and that stuff told me it was the way to escape, and that I was gonna be somebody. Finally, I was somebody. But it tricked me, and it keeps tricking me. Kept me helpless all these years, telling I'm going to escape out of here, and that I'm going to make it to the American dream. *(waves his hands*

*together up in the air as if he is revealing something.)* I chased that dream, but I never knew how to reach it. Too late for old Parker; yup, that's what they say. *(looks at the floor)* I'm Bob Parker. Here's my ID. *He puts his ID on the staff counter.*

Pearl: *(quiet for a few moments, but her nonverbal language is accepting)* It's never too late for anyone. *Bob Parker looks up at Pearl with surprise. There is silence as Pearl and Bob Parker look at each other. Then Bob Parker smiles at Pearl.* These forms have to be filled out. My name is Pearl. Please ask me any questions you have.

Bob Parker: Pearl? Like a pearl in an oyster? My grandfather was a pearl farming hand ages ago. It's hard to find pearls in the open waters anymore, many have to be cultured on farms. The transparent pearls are the ones of value, you know? Can see right through them—means they have a good crystal structure. *(pause)* It's all in how things appear that make the value. Defective pearls are dull, the structure's all messed up inside, you can't see through them at all, and they make some real wild shapes. *(pauses for a few seconds)* Isn't it amazing that some pearls develop perfect crystal structures and some don't? *(pause)* Well, I guess it's not much of a mystery though. Comes down to the shell environment, all about the right chemistry in the shell. The right chemistry in the shell makes a valuable pearl.

Pearl: *(nods her head)* Yeah, but we need to get better at finding the beauty in the wild ones, right?

Bob Parker: *(smiles and laughs)* Now you made me laugh. Thank you, Pearl. *(puts his head down)* I'm going to tackle these forms.

Narrator: People need to be listened to; just really listened to. No judgement. Cause being listened to empowers people.

*Narrator picks up the guitar and is strumming it in the waiting area. Bob Parker turns and sits down in the waiting room and is working on the forms on the device.*

Narrator: *(stops playing the guitar)* Wait, hear that? *(laughing is heard)* It's faint. It's coming from behind the green glass doors. Pearl hears it.

*Narrator walks with the guitar and moves closer to the green glass door.*

*Pearl has a concerned look on her face. Bob Parker gets up and is standing, waiting for Pearl.*

Bob Parker: I might need some extra time to finish these forms.

Pearl: *(feeling anxious that he might hear the laughing)* Don't worry about it. Have a seat, Mr. Parker. We'll be with you soon. I'm going to call Dr. Mark.

*Mr. Parker goes back to the chairs to sit down.*
*There is sarcastic laughing from behind the green glass doors. Pearl is trying to reach James on the phone, without luck.*

Pearl: *(to Mary the intern)* There they go again, always laughing. Stay here, Mary. I'm going to get James.

*Pearl walks through the green glass doors to James' desk. Narrator follows Pearl.*

Narrator: Followers like to pull in more followers. Why? It justifies their choice to follow in the first place. No one likes to laugh alone.

Rosy: Pearl, we can't believe old Parker finally came back. After all these years. Talk about cyclers; he was at the top of the list in his younger years. What a frequent flyer! Some things never change.

Claire: *(in a mocking tone imitating Bob Parker)* The system made me helpless. *(laughing)* Yeah, right. How about all that booze? That man will never change.

Pearl: I need to get Dr. Mark.

Claire: There is nothing wrong with that man. He probably picked up the cane for a prop.

Stella: Makes it look like the system beat him down. Now he has a cane. *(laughing)*

*Pearl speaks softly, and her voice is rather shaky; her shyness is apparent, but she is firm in her message.*

Pearl: We like to help the people who get better. If they get better, that comes back to us. We're the magician that changed their lives. *(pauses)* Helping someone is the hardest when they don't change, when it doesn't work out, when you're not the hero.

*The welfare workers and Claire respond by making surprised, mocking faces. James walks in, and the welfare workers quickly switch to more neutral faces and start to return to their desks.*

Pearl: James, Mr. Bob Parker is here and has a cane. He is asking for you.

*Claire is still standing in the same place, staring Pearl down.*

Claire: Go ahead, Dr. Mark; go fix him up *(with a mocking face)*— again. *(She turns and walks away with a dismissive face.)*

*James ignores Claire in a firm, dismissive way. James looks at Pearl in a supportive way. Pearl smiles softly at James and seems to welcome his comfort. Pearl heads through the green glass doors, and James follows.*

Pearl: Mr. Parker. *Mr. Parker gets out of his chair and comes to the staff counter.* Go with Dr. Mark. You can finish the forms with him.

James: Hello, Mr. Parker. What's with the cane?

Mr. Parker: Just need it for a little balance, that's all. Helps my leg along. I was lucky to find the cane. There it was in the trash just when I needed it. Like it fell from heaven.

James: Well, I'm glad that you found one. You know we could've gotten you one?

Mr. Parker: Yes, I know. But I like to take care of myself if I can. Only ask for help if it's absolutely necessary. That's what this here system taught me. Cause if you ask for help too much you might get what you didn't ask for. And then you're really trapped.

James: *smiles and nods at Mr. Parker.*

*James and Mr. Parker head through the green glass doors. Pearl continues working. The waiting room is full of clients. James and Mr. Parker and Mike soon emerge from the green glass doors.*

Mr. Parker: *(headed towards front doors with Mike and talking to James)* Well, if you say tests, I'll do it. But only because you said it.

*Mike and Bob Parker exit.*
*James walks over to Pearl to give her the half-completed forms on the tablet.*

Pearl: We can probably get some of the information from the last time he was here. Are the tests for his leg?

James: No. Might be some arthritis in his leg, but the liver is the bigger problem. The alcohol is taking a toll now. *(quiet for a few seconds.)* So any plans for this weekend? How about a day trip somewhere?

Pearl: Oh, I'm tired. I don't think so.

James: *(with passion)* We need an escape from this. There's no end to this misery. There must be a better system. At least more compassionate people? How will Mr. Parker be helped?

Pearl: *(passionate back)* I don't know. It's so discouraging. Makes me so angry.

James: What stirs such judgment in people?

Pearl: I don't know. But judgment squashes any room for hope.

Narrator: The day has come to its end. The people in the waiting room are gathering to get the vans.

*One of the green glass doors opens, and Claire appears.*

Claire: Here, Pearl. Final placements. I made sure to add correctly. *(sarcastic tone and leaves)*

James: OK, well, I'll let you finish up. Call me in the morning with some plans? Your trips always help to revive me. *(James smiles with seriousness at Pearl.)*

Pearl: *(smiles back)* I know you too well, James. You're trying to guilt me into this. Stop with those serious faces. OK?
*James turns to go back through the green glass doors and smirks at Pearl, and Pearl smirks back in a playful way.*

*Van and bus numbers are called from an offstage voice. Kids are jumping everywhere, excited to be out of the waiting area. As Pearl turns to close the front door for the last client, a gust of wind comes from behind her and shuts the front doors behind her. She heads through the green glass doors to get her belongings to leave for the day. Pearl exits the front doors and stands by a bus sign.*

Narrator: Pearl is taking the bus today. *Narrator talks as Pearl and the other people wait at the bus-stop sign.* The buses are getting crowded lately. There are laws in the city about when you can drive. See the signs up there? Even license plate numbers Monday, Wednesday, Friday. Odd numbers on Tuesdays and Thursdays. Traffic and congestion are a constant issue. Carpooling even has to be enforced. Did you know that carpooling gives people breaks on their income taxes? It's like having another child if you carpool. Ok, I am digressing from the story, but I just had to add that in. We are in the future, you know. *Narrator strolls away, and stage lights fade to black.*

### Act 4, scene 1: June: a Saturday, the importance of the moment

*While the narrator is talking, Pearl is walking on the stage. There are church bells ringing in the distance.*

Narrator: Can you hear the noon church bells ringing? There aren't too many churches left to play those noon bells. *(sound of buzzing gnat)* And hear that gnat buzzing in Pearl's face? As if to say, "Pay attention." The church bells, the gnats, the sounds of the day that bring attention to the importance of the moment. That moment in the everyday that you don't realize is important at the time. But it is.

*Lights onstage go out except for a light on Pearl and the narrator. The church bells are still ringing.*

*A stage light appears in the corner of the stage on Pearl's mother at a kitchen table. Young Pearl is sitting on the ground playing nearby.*

Narrator: Pearl, age four. Hear the noon church bells ringing? The importance of the moment. Pearl's mother is making lunch. Peanut butter and jelly sandwiches and grapes. And there's Pearl's faded memory of her mother's voice, calling her name.

Pearl's Mother: Pearl, lunch.

*Stage light dims in the corner of the stage, and then the stage lights come back to present scene.*
*Pearl sees her elderly neighbor, Ms. Anne. A sign appears from the ceiling that reads, "The Great Depression, featuring Dorothea Lange".*

Ms. Anne: Hello, Pearl.

Pearl: *(distracted from the flashback)* Hello, Ms. Anne. Doing your errands?

Ms. Anne: Well, you could say that. At my age, I need to get out every day, even if I'm making up errands. *(Both laugh.)* What are you up to?

Pearl: *(points to sign)* I'm headed to the Great Depression show to meet friends. Would you like to come?

Ms. Anne: Well, that's kind of you. That does sound interesting. You know, I'll take you up on your offer.

Pearl: Great.

*Pearl and Ms. Anne start walking towards the sign; people enter and exit stage as if walking on the street. Luke enters the stage behind Pearl and Ms.Anne.*

Luke: *(waving rather excitedly for Luke)* Pearl!

*Pearl turns and seems surprised by Luke's excitement.*

Pearl: *(warm smile)* Hi, Luke *(quickly turns to Ms. Anne)*. Ms. Anne, this is Luke Matthews, a friend of mine.

Ms. Anne: Nice to meet you.

Luke: You too.

*A stage light appears in the corner, a projection of a Catholic church appears on the back wall. A few protesters enter stage, holding signs in front of the image. The signs read "Support Sr.*

*Carmela!" Protesters are yelling, "Sr. Carmela, save our churches!*
*"Women leaders in the church!".*

Luke: Have you heard about Sr. Carmela? *(turns to Pearl)*

Pearl: Oh, aren't they saying she's holding the Catholic churches together? Ordaining deacons? Conducting masses, and funerals?

Luke: Yeah, that's the rumor. But no one wants to confirm it. My new research is about the closing Christian churches. I'd love to interview her. Some call her Carmela of Arc.

Ms. Anne: It's about time a woman took on the Catholic church. Never thought I'd see it in my life. *(pause)* I'm Presbyterian. I remember when younger generations stopped going to my church. Families focused their time on kids sports and dance activities. It was sad to see my church close.

Pearl: After my mother died, my father made us go to our Baptist church every Sunday. Said we could feel closer to my mother there. I don't go to church anymore. But sometimes I sit in an empty church. It's peaceful.

Luke: Well, my parents were never around to make us go to church. They traveled a lot with their government jobs. My sister and I were raised by nannies. They divorced civilly when I was fifteen. But my mother had a strong faith; she had some relatives from Syria who were Eastern Catholics that influenced her. So, she did have my sister and I confirmed in the Catholic Church.

Pearl: *(nods).*

Luke: My faith feels like a badge I earned in eighth grade when I was confirmed. I have an eighth-grade faith. *(laughs)*

Pearl: *(laughs and then pauses)* Any faith I have comes from the church music I sang as a kid.

Luke: Really?

Pearl: *(clears her throat and sings)* We will work with each other, we will work side by side, we will work with each other, we will work side by side, and we'll guard each one's dignity and save each one's pride *(laughs)*

Luke: *(smiles)* You have a nice voice.

Pearl: *(blushes and laughs)* Well, I guess. *(smiles)*

Ms. Anne: When I sang that as a child it was guard each *man's* dignity and save each *man's* pride. *(smiles and laughs)*
*Pearl and Luke laugh.*
*Pearl appears less guarded with Luke.*

Luke: Well, you know, younger generations have abandoned Christian churches. Ideas about eternal damnation and mortal sins, all the guilt and shame, it's unappealing to them. And the new generations don't need churches for community. They have sports teams, the arts, and of course, social media. You don't have to gather in person anymore, with all the virtual community going on.

Pearl: I'd like to see it when it's finished.

Ms. Anne: Pearl, you will let me know when it's on?

Pearl: Sure Ms. Anne.

*Pearl, Ms. Anne, and Luke stop walking. Three large photos appear from the ceiling and some other smaller pictures are projected on standing white boards. Ryan and his fiancé, Marie, enter stage and stand in front of one of Lange's pictures. James enters stage standing in the distance looking at a picture. Pearl, Luke and Ms. Anne approach Ryan and Marie and greet them.*

Marie: I had relatives from Japan who lived in California. They were sent to internments. I'm surprised they finally circulated these pictures. History was so altered by government censorship back then. Well, it probably is today too. We just don't know it.

Pearl: Yeah, the lives of the Japanese Americans are still overlooked from that era. When something gets locked into history, it often stays that way.

*James turns, sees Ms. Anne looking at a small photo, and goes over and hugs her. A waiter is going by and James asks for a drink.*

Ms. Anne: James, it's good to see you. *(looking at an elderly Japanese woman in a picture)* The elderly struggled so much back then. But I feel for the elderly people today too. I was lucky; my husband had one of the rare jobs with a pension. But many were not as lucky as me.

James: *(Nods his head in agreement)* How are you feeling these days?

Ms. Anne: Oh, not terrible. Thanks for asking. This arthritis gives me problems, but I keep up my exercises. *Ms. Anne looks in the distance behind James.* Excuse me, James; there's a restroom. My old bladder is calling. *(They smile and laugh.)*

*Ms. Anne heads off stage briefly. The waiter finds James and hands him a drink from his tray. James walks over to Pearl, who is standing in front of a picture of a closed New York bank from the Great Depression era.*

James: I can't imagine what that was like. All your cash instantly gone. *(grimaces and slips his drink.)*

Pearl: Yeah, that must've been scary. The New Deal was a great idea. Took us out of the Great Depression. But no one ever monitored that system. No wonder the old welfare system crashed. *(pause)*

*Pearl and James start studying one of the large pictures hanging from the ceiling, a picture of a poor family from the Great Depression. Luke approaches with Ms. Anne, as well as Ryan and Marie.*

Pearl: What were their lives like? Was this a close, loving family due to poverty, or did poverty rip them apart?

*A light appears, narrator starts playing the guitar. Three characters enter stage in the front corner and start singing: Bob Parker, Ronald Johnson, and Anthony [sign Tracy Chapman Talkin'Bout A Revolution]. Narrator eventually joins in signs as he plays the guitar. The white boards are removed from the stage, the pictures from the ceiling are pulled up, and the stage is empty.*

*The singing is all that is heard. We see Pearl, Luke, and Ms. Anne say good-bye to the other characters and the other characters exit the stage. The three walk past the singing characters and begin walking around as if back on the street. Ms. Anne says good-bye and heads offstage. Pearl and Luke are left together, about to part ways. The singing fades away, signing characters exit stage.*

Pearl: *(short silence)* Hey, good luck on the documentary.

Luke: Thanks.

*Pearl smiles and starts to turn away but stops.*

Pearl: You know sometimes even a documentary can't capture the whole story at an agency. Most people don't tell you the real stuff going on.

Luke: Yeah, I get it. It's hard to capture the true story. People aren't going to tell you everything if they could lose their job. Especially in this economy.

Pearl: We have to "measure" all the services given to people. *(mocking)* Numbers show accountability. The funny thing is, makes it much easier to make up stuff. Just check off you provided a service, add the numbers up, no one checks if it really happened.

Luke: I know. Numbers rule everything now, and sometimes not for the better.

Pearl: Some days I think I should find another place to work rather than try to fight a place with problems. But I keep thinking it's really everywhere.

Luke: *(smiles and makes a face like he doesn't know)*

Pearl: *(looking off into the distance, seems a little distracted)* Well the show inspired me. Makes me get ideas. Ideas like I can change things someday.

Luke: Um, yes. *(nods and looks away)* You know, I have to be honest, I don't get what you're talking about.

Pearl: *(surprised but interested)* Oh. really?

Luke: Well, I appreciate the art. They're great photos.

Pearl: *(makes a dismissive face at Luke and with passion)* What about the human desperation? Couldn't you connect to any of that?

Luke: Not really. But it's interesting to hear you talk. *(pauses and looks away a little timidly, which is out of character for Luke)* You give things a different view, especially when it comes to the poor. A view I couldn't have found myself—something I still don't understand.

Pearl: Oh. *(pauses and is quiet)* Well, I try to put myself in other people's shoes, understand what they must've gone through. It helps me appreciate what I have. It's so easy in America to focus on building my own happiness, always seeking to get what I don't have.

Luke: *(smiles and picks up his foot and studies his shoe)* I guess I need to try out some different shoes once in a while.
*Pearl laughs at the way Luke picks up his shoe and seems surprised by his openness.*

Luke: Enjoy the weekend. See you around. *(turns to leave)*

Pearl: Oh, OK. Yeah, see you later.

*Pearl and Luke look back at each other, smile, and then exit stage in different directions.*

**Act 4, scene 2: June: Welfare Intake Office Q, a hot and humid Wednesday**

*There are people gathering outside the front doors. It's hot and humid at 8:50 a.m. Pearl opens the doors early. The children run in. John Roberts approaches Claire as she is entering the front doors. He is pacing behind her. John is very sweaty due to the weather, and also he is talking and moving quickly. He follows Claire through the front doors into the waiting room. He is in his mid-twenties.*

Claire: *(with an impatient tone)* What do you want? I can't understand you. *(She keeps walking.)*

*Claire approaches Pearl, who is standing in the waiting room.*

Claire: I'm not sure what this man wants. He's acting like he's somebody important, but he's making no sense. He's probably high or something. Call Dr. Mark.

*Pearl walks past Claire and gets a cup of water from the cooler.*

John: *(walks up to Claire again as she is trying to flee to the green glass doors)* Excuse me. Do you know where room thirty-six is? I have an important meeting there. I need to be there.

Claire: Here. Tell Pearl. *Claire points to Pearl and walks away through the green glass doors.*

Pearl: Come sit for a moment. Would you like some water? It's very hot outside this morning.

John: I don't have time. I need to get to room thirty-six. Do you know where that is?

Pearl: What's your name? *She attempts to talk to him and at the same time is calling Dr. Mark.*

John: *(starts calling on phone and says to Pearl)* Yes, finally I reached someone *(on the phone)* Hello, where is room thirty-six located? I'm going to be late for the meeting. This is John Roberts.

Person: *(on the phone)* Sorry, who is this? What meeting? *(call disconnects)*

John: Oh, I just lost the connection.

Pearl: Is your name John Roberts? Did you need welfare housing? Or medical services?

John: Oh, yes. But I need to go to my meeting first.

Pearl: I'll put the water here. *Pearl places the cup of water on the small table near the chair.*
 Someone is coming to help you.

*John decides to take a sip of the water. Claire comes through the green doors to greet some movers coming in the front doors with a leather sofa. James comes through the green glass doors behind her.*

Claire: Oh, look how beautiful it is! And it was free, free! *Claire is rubbing her hands on the leather sofa and examining it while the movers are holding the sofa.*

John: *(turns to Claire once he sees that she is present again in the waiting area)* I don't think you heard me before. I need to get to my meeting.

Claire: *(annoyed)* I told you to talk to Pearl. I'm busy.

*James quickly engages John, and redirects him from Claire and her sofa. Claire continues to direct the movers through the green glass doors toward her office. She creates a big commotion trying to prop open the green glass doors and angle the sofa through them. The commotion overpowers the other characters until the green glass doors swing shut.*

James: This way, John? *James walks him through the green glass doors. James turns back to Pearl as the door is closing behind him and talks quickly. (turns to Pearl)* Pearl, I'll do a finger scan and see what comes up. Not sure where to send him. *(Pearl nods.)*

Narrator: People with *mental illness* are not always welcome at the Welfare Department Store Housing sites. People are afraid of an illness they don't understand. I think we create the fear and misunderstanding by giving people labels in the first place. Mentally ill, really? Who came up with that one? We create the boundaries amongst ourselves.

*Pearl notices Claire and James talking behind the green glass doors. She can't hear them speaking. The narrator walks through the green glass doors to where Claire and James are standing. Now we hear Claire and James.*

James: *(raises his voice in anger)* Some of the most intelligent people I have met have mental illnesses. He had a significant position at a well-known company. Impressed now? We never listen to the mentally ill. *(very sarcastic)* Just medicate them. Give them their injections. They don't make "sense," right?

*Claire makes an angry face and walks away.*

*James goes back to John in his office. James is able to get him to take some medication and walks him to the waiting area. John continues calling on his phone.*

Narrator: These days you can't send the poor with mental health symptoms to the emergency room, and you can't hospitalize them. There's no money to pay for it. Science made it easier to "control" mental health symptoms with injections. Give them an injection and send them on their way.

*James returns to his desk. He pauses and looks up.*

*Stage lights fade to black. There is a spotlight on James and the narrator. A light appears in a dark corner of the stage. Young James, age seven, is walking around with his mother in an imaginary park together. There is a flute player softly playing in the background.*

Narrator: James, age seven.

James's Mother: *(happily laughing and skipping in an impulsive and overly energetic manner and talking rapidly)* Hurry, James. Come on. We need to get to the zoo. The sea lions won't wait for us. Hurry, hurry. Hear the sea lions? They're calling us. Do you hear them, sweetie? They are singing to us. How beautifully they sing. And they are telling us to hurry or we will miss them. I am coming, seals. *James's mother disappears from Young James's sight.*

Young James: Mother, Mother, where are you? *James is happy and running around, trying to find where his mother went; eventually he sees her in the distance and runs after her.*

Narrator: Young James was excited to have his mother paying attention to him. She wasn't locked in her bedroom. His mom was full of energy today.

*Light fades away on Young James and his mother. Stage goes black. Flute stops. Then stage lights gradually come back on James in the present.*

Pearl: *(calling in on phone)* James?

James: Yes?

Pearl: John is leaving.

James: *(runs out through the green glass doors)* Wait, John. Stay here for a bit and prepare for your meeting. It's hot out.

John: Well for a few more minutes. *(He starts to type very quickly on his phone.)*

Pearl: How about some old-fashioned paper and pen? *(Pearl hands paper and pens John.)*

John: Ah, I haven't seen those in a long time. The government keeps that stuff to themselves.
*He starts writing with the pen on the paper, looking from time to time at the pen, examining it.*

*Jane walks through the front doors with her overdramatic bubbly happiness. She looks around and notices John typing at high speeds and then writing with the pen on the paper. Jane walks over to Pearl.*

Jane: *(with exaggerated concern)* Pearl, this man looks anxious. You need to do something.

Pearl: *(frustrated)* Yes, Jane. Dr. Mark is working on it.

Jane: Oh, OK. *(glances around.)* It's busy, so make sure you check everyone in.

Pearl: Yes, Jane. *(forced smile)*

Jane: *(glances at a book on the counter)* What's this? Oh, Crime and Punishment? Are you reading this, Pearl? That's a great psychological novel. What was that about? I don't remember.

Pearl: A man who justified killing an inconsiderate woman, all in the name of social justice.

Jane: Oh, yes. Imagine justifying killing a person.

Pearl: I guess people create the realities they want to believe.

Jane: Yes, I know. It's so sad. The people we serve just don't see their problems. Such denial. Always justifying their poor decisions.

Narrator: Well, I guess Jane Bidding is exempt. *(sarcastically)* She truly knows herself. *Narrator gesturing at the clients sitting in the chairs.* These poor people. What's wrong with them?

*Pearl doesn't look up at Jane and ignores her comment and continues working.*

Jane: Well, I need to get back to work.

*Jane goes through the green glass doors, and as soon as they shut, we see Mr. Blunt walk through the front doors. He starts wandering around the waiting room, talking with people.*

Mr. Blunt: Hello, you look busy today. *(to John)*

John: Yes, preparing for my meeting. *(puts out his hand to shake)* John Roberts.

Mr. Blunt: Nice to meet you, John. Good luck there.
*He pauses and walks over to Pearl at the staff area.*

Mr. Blunt: Hello, Pearl. Busy day today. Keep up the good work.

Pearl: Yes, thanks. *Pearl looks up only briefly, smiles at Mr. Blunt, and continues working.*

Narrator: Look at the child over there. *(there is a child playing on the small carpet)* What will his life be like when he grows up? What choices will he have?
*Narrator walks back over to Pearl and looks over her shoulder.*
Claire's numbers still don't add up. Still a bit of cheating going on with those stats. Who's really benefiting from the high numbers? *(shrugs his shoulders).* I guess Pearl didn't accomplish much from her confrontation with Claire?
Well, she did gain one thing: confidence—something every young person needs to take on the world. *(pause)* People live in their own realities. Pearl couldn't smash Claire's reality.
The corrupt bureaucracy is led by corrupt administrators. Well, let's not smash Mr. Blunt entirely. OK, yes, he sometimes might make some shady deals with landlords, but, hey, that's in the name of social justice, right? The problem with Mr. Blunt is that he wants to believe everyone is doing a great job and there are no problems in his agency. Corrupt? I don't know. Definitely not effective. But,

again, not Pearl's job to smash his reality. What's Pearl's reality? *(writes on the whiteboard next to the other words from the beginning of the play)* "Compassion." "Hope." Someday she'll overpower America with those. *Narrator points to the words on the whiteboard: "American dream," "status," "power," "money," "conquer," "hope," and "compassion." Narrator goes back and taps "compassion" a few times and nods his head and smiles.*

*John leaves with someone that James called. The office is busy, and there is a lot of commotion, but everyone continues with their jobs.*

Narrator: *(slowly turns the wall clock hands to show the passing of the hours of the day)*
Well, another day ends. Mr. Blunt left around noon for a business lunch. He never came back. Jane Bidding had a luncheon on healthcare issues for the poor. She didn't come back either. Claire's on the phone, sitting on her "free" sofa. I think a family crisis, but I'm not sure.

*Pearl is gathering her belongings, and James comes through the green glass doors.*

James: Hey, you heading out? I'll walk with you.

Pearl: Yeah, all set.

*Pearl and James exit the front doors and start walking in silence on stage. Narrator follows them.*

Narrator: The warmth of the summer sun and the fresh air are so satisfying after a day indoors.

*Pearl and James go to a bench and sit down. Both are sitting on the bench facing outward and staring into space as if tired. Narrator is standing nearby.*

Narrator: *(points to recreated tree branches hanging on sticks over the characters)* The tree branches are hanging like fans of green. The branches seem to be celebrating as they wave in the soft, warm breeze. The birds are calling to each other as they fly overhead. *(points to the fake birds flying overhead)*

Pearl: So many needs today.

James: So many needs with no solutions. *The birds are calling above them, and that is all that can be heard for ten seconds.* John reminded me of my mother.

Pearl: Oh?

James: She had episodes like that when I was a kid. *(James's phone rings.)* Hello? Yes, my call starts in fifteen minutes. Yes, I'll take the case. Good-bye.
*(before Pearl can respond)* Well, back to work. Call starting. *(He gets up from the bench.)*
*(He turns around.)* I don't think I ever told anyone that before. About my mother.

Pearl: Oh. *(smiles softly)*

James: See you tomorrow. *(walks away several feet and turns back around)* Ah, Pearl? *(pauses while Pearl looks up at him)* Oh, forget it. I better go.

*James walks away; he turns around in the distance, pauses and looks at Pearl, and then waves. Pearl waves back and watches him walk off stage.*

*Pearl gets up from the bench and starts walking.*

Narrator: *Narrator nods toward the distance.* The church groups are out making their rounds to the commuters.

*Pearl walks past a church person who is speaking in a loud, clear voice with a megaphone.*

Church Person: Remember the words of Mother Teresa: "Joy is prayer, joy is strength, joy is love, joy is the net of life, by which we catch others. God loves a cheerful giver; in the service of God and others, it is always hard to be joyful" Did you hear that? "In the service of God and others, it's always hard to be joyful."

*Church person repeats the last part of the quote over and over. Pearl exits the stage. We hear the last part of the quote as the stage lights go black.*

**Act 4, scene 3: late August, Ryan and Marie's wedding**

*Stage lights up. A projected image of a church can be seen on the backstage wall. Set has chairs that form an aisle, a podium, there are vases of zinnias and hydrangeas and a freestanding stained-glass window. Narrator is strolling around the stage.*

Narrator: Ryan and Marie's wedding. August thirty-first. It's a sticky, hot, end-of-summer day. The grass has lost its green luster. The summer flowers have mostly died. Oh, but wait—not the zinnias. *Narrator points dramatically to the zinnias.* Look at those tall zinnias, bright pink, cranberry, and yellow. They stand tall. *Narrator excitedly walks over to the hydrangeas.* And the hydrangeas—still grabbing attention, having turned from their summer blue to their end-of-summer deep maroon. So hard to find hydrangeas blooming these days.

*Narrator approaches set, and sits in a chair. Most of the chairs are filled. Music starts, and modern dancers appear and dance in the aisle of the church briefly. As the music fades, the dancers exit the stage. Ryan and Marie are at the podium.*

*Stage lights fade out.*
*Stage lights come on.*

*It's after the wedding ceremony. The chairs are empty. Ryan and Marie are taking pictures, they are gathered in the back of the stage, outside the set. Children in dress clothes are running around. Everyone is gathered around them except Pearl.*

*Pearl is wandering in the set chairs by herself. The narrator is watching.*

Narrator: Nothing more peaceful than an empty church. Look at that beautiful stained-glass window.

*There is light projecting through the stained glass and sending colors of light dancing around the stage. Luke approaches the set and the empty chairs.*

Luke: *(speaking to Pearl with an eagerness that is out of character for Luke)* I wondered where you went. I wanted to tell you more about the documentary.

Pearl: Yeah, sure.

*Narrator picks up a nearby guitar and starts strumming softly in the background. Luke speaks as he slowly walks towards Pearl.*

Luke: Did you know that churches stayed afloat by renting out their basement halls for weddings? Young people coming out of college had huge college loans and couldn't afford fancy wedding facilities.

Pearl: I kinda remember reading about that. *(pauses and is twirling around in the aisle)* That dance was beautiful before, don't you think?

*Pearl does a large spin to try to imitate a dance move. She doesn't realize that Luke is that close to her in the aisle. She bumps into him, and blushes. They stop and look at each other. They forget their conversation, at first looking rather skeptically at each other, but then feeling drawn to each other. They both freeze in the scene for a moment, when the narrator speaks.*

Narrator: Life is funny. One small, unexpected move can make someone change his or her course in life and then the courses of other lives around them. Did you just hear what I said? One small, unexpected move, yup just one.

Pearl: I don't understand you. *(pause)* You're so judgmental. You have no compassion toward people. *(pause)* But I guess you don't pretend to be compassionate. *(pause)* You're honest about it.

Narrator: Oh, Luke's hidden quality: honesty. Didn't quite see it till now.

Luke: *(quiet for a moment)* I like how you feel about people. It fascinates me. *(pause)* You fascinate me. (*with a desirous look on his face).* You get me to look at the world differently. Something I never learned till I met you.

*Pearl: (surprised and emotional) Oh.*

Luke: I grew up on my own. Emotions weren't needed; they just got in the way. Kept me from succeeding. But you taught me that emotions are needed, really needed.

Pearl: Oh. *(pauses)* I lost my mother when I was a child. My father always encouraged us to care for others. I guess it was his way of dealing with his own sorrow. Giving to others was his comfort and that's what I learned to do.

*They stare at each other briefly, and kiss. They stop and look at each other and smile. They grab each other's hands to exit the church set. Around them, a rainbow of colors streams through the stained-glass windows.*

Narrator: Ah, the unity of America, perhaps? *(smiles and nods at the couple)*

*Narrator is behind Pearl and Luke.*
*A park bench is moved on stage in the back.*

Narrator: *(picks up a dead, brown leaf and holds it up, examining it)*
The beauty of fall is creeping in. Fall is a time of death through
magnificent colors. The fall colors usher in the barrenness of winter.
And then comes spring, the hope of new beginnings. Summer is the
vibrancy and beauty of nature celebrating. What a beautiful cycle of
life the four seasons are.
*Narrator points towards back stage.* Wait, who's that stumbling
along? Pearl knows him. That's Mr. Bob Parker.

*Bob Parker appears to be stumbling as if intoxicated and sits down
on the bench.*

Pearl: How do you reverse a lifetime of wrong choices? When all
your good at is failing, how can you believe things will ever change?

*Luke looks at Bob Parker, but is unsure what Pearl is talking about.*

Narrator: Well, he can't do it alone, that's for sure. You have no
confidence in yourself after a lifetime of wrong choices. Nope. No
confidence. None.

Pearl: He started out as someone's child. A long time ago, he was
someone's child.

*Luke is looking from Pearl to Mr. Parker with confusion.*

Narrator: Luke is trying to understand what Pearl is talking about.
He wants to understand, but he's still confused. *(pause)* Look at Mr.
Parker, he's enjoying the sun. The fading summer sunbeams
surround him and provide a glimmer of hope *(lights are shining on
Mr. Parker)* as glimpses of fall begin to blow around him. *Narrator*

*points to blowing, dead, brown leaves around Mr. Parker's feet.* The only few dead leaves of the approaching fall are blowing around his feet.

*All stage lights fade away, and the last stage lights left are shining just on Mr. Parker on the bench. Then those lights fade out, and the stage goes dark.*

## *Epilogue: Fall, October 2002*

*The narrator is sitting outside on a bench near the front doors.*

Narrator: Ah, autumn. Look at that color. *(Narrator points to many red, vibrant leaves blowing around.)* So, there you have it. A story about the future. Yes, we were in the future. Maybe 2035? I don't know; you pick a year. *(smiles)* But we're back in the present now: 2002. Were you listening? I said 2002. I work for this office, the Department of Social Services, DSS. But, you know maybe my future story was not so far from your present life? Think about it. Gotta go.

*Narrator enters the front doors. He goes through the green glass doors and hangs his coat and hat up on a hook. Then he returns through the green glass doors and walks toward the staff area.*

Narrator: The waiting room looks familiar, right? There are those huge, solid, green glass doors. The fluorescent light is shorting out. Limited technology, though; it's only 2002 in a county welfare office. Only the old dinosaur computers. And the whiteboards are in full use in 2002. *(points to the detailed schedules on the boards and tons of papers hanging around)* Paper galore.

*A young man walks in the main front doors. It's a young Roy Blunt.*

Narrator: Hello there, Roy. How's it going?

Roy: Good, Kier. It's going to be busy today. I'm eager to hear the new requirements. Hope the forms are more user-friendly.

Narrator: Should be interesting.

Roy: Yup, Kier. Change is good.

*Roy goes through the green glass doors, hangs up his coat and hat. There are corded desk phones and big computer monitors sitting on the desks. Roy comes back to the waiting area and sits next to the narrator at the staff counter.*

Roy: So, I was meaning to ask you: is Kier your full name?

Narrator: Kier is short for Kierkegaard. Kierkegaard is my full name. I'm named after the famous philosopher, Kierkegaard.

Roy: Really? Who's that?

Narrator: I don't know; but that's what happens when you have a mother who's a college philosophy professor. Damn parents, they scar you for life. *Both laugh out loud.*
*Narrator walks over to the copier and starts examining it, pulling papers out.* Someone left the copier jammed from yesterday. Well, it's the start of a regular day, Roy.

Roy: Yup. Can't start the day without fixing yesterday's copier jam.

*Roy walks over and unlocks the front doors. Adult clients and children enter the waiting room. The clients and children all sit in the chairs. One by one, the adult clients and children stand up and take turns speaking the following lines [this will be to instrumental music]:*

Clients: America's future will bring many new changes: new welfare systems, new political changes and world conflicts, new pollutions, new technology, new diseases, new creatures through evolution, new extinct creatures, changing sea levels, unpredictable weather patterns.

*They remain standing. Margaret Brown stands up.*

Margaret Brown: But the past and the future are not so different when we realize that the need for hope is something that never changes over time.

*Ronald P. Johnson stands up.*

Ronald P. Johnson: And the past tells us that hope is something that is worked for; it doesn't just happen.

*John Roberts stands up.*

John: Hope is not magical. Hope is determination.

*Mrs. Baxter stands up.*

Mrs. Baxter: Hope is not whimsical. Hope is courage.

*Mr. Parker stands up.*

Mr. Bob Parker: Hope is believing that there is hidden beauty in the defective pearls. Hope is something we can give to each other. Hope in each other can become the new American dream.

*All the adult clients and children grasp hands and lift their hands up together. Narrator grabs the guitar and starts off the song: If I Had a Hammer Trini Lopez version. Bob Parker leads the singing and starts dancing and clapping. Cast all sing and dance together in the waiting room, jumping on waiting room chairs and dancing excitedly. Song ends.*

*Stage lights go out.*